IMPERFECT DIVINE

A SHADE OF MIND
BOOK FOUR

OUTLANDERS OF THE MULTIVERSE
COLLECTION

BY D.N. LEO

Narrative Land Publishing
Narrativeland.com

A Shade of Mind Series
Www.narrativeland.com/shade

1-4 Random Psychic
2-4 Forever Mortal
3-4 Elusive Beings
4-4 Imperfect Divine

IMPERFECT DIVINE

Synopsis

Ciaran and Madeline haven't chosen power. Power comes with great responsibility. They'd rather fight for happiness. And Eudaiz is the universe that offers them just that. Happiness.

But to be in Eudaiz and save the lives of millions, they must pass the Daimon Gate tests—the most stringent tests of bravery and worthiness. Tests they might not survive to see the light of happiness they long for.

This final installment in an urban fantasy thriller series, filled with romance and science fiction twists and turns, will take you to the heart of those who dare to embrace the dark side of human mind.

PROLOGUE

Her high heels clicked on the hard cold cobblestones of the dark alley. The unpleasant sound echoed back and forth between the narrow stone fences along the sides of the road. Fog crept up from the ground and brushed her long legs that the thermal stockings didn't give much warmth to.

She regretted taking this shortcut already.

But at the other end of this alley, a surprise birthday party was waiting for her. Well, not really much of a surprise since she knew about it. Her best friend had tipped her off by asking her to wear something nice for their girls' night out.

She smiled to herself and tried to ignore the eerie ambiance surrounding her. She was turning eighteen.

Soon.

She heard the sound of flapping wings. This area was notorious for bats—one of those animals she didn't care much for. It had to be an enormous bat by the sound of it. She looked up but saw nothing but the dark sky.

She put her head down and kept walking, pulling out her cell phone to call her friends. No signal. "I'm in the middle of the town, for God's sake!" she cursed to no one in particular and picked up her pace.

Her footsteps echoed louder and louder in the dark alley. Or maybe it was just in her head.

But she wasn't hearing her footsteps now. She was hearing someone else's. She turned around, but there was nothing but a long, dark alley. Reaching the other end where she could see a dim light would be faster than going back.

She could see traffic and pedestrians in the distance. Seeing people made her feel a lot better. She kept walking.

Suddenly, the metallic stench of blood engulfed her. It was so overwhelming she had to gasp to draw in air. The shadow of a man stepped out in front of her, from . . . nowhere. He cast a glance at her with his flaming red eyes. And he smirked.

It was a smirk of victory and satisfaction as if he had just found a long lost treasure.

She froze. She wasn't scared. She didn't pass out. She just couldn't move.

Then a cold blast of air invaded her. It felt like ants crawling all over her body. Her mind was numb. Something was clawing at her soul, seeping into every cell of her body, ripping the dignity out of her.

Every thought she had in her mind. All of her secrets. All aspects of her life. Everything was exposed.

All of her memories of her sweet childhood, of her friends, of her family were leaving her. Bit by bit. The pain in her heart was unbearable.

She was fully awake, lying on the cold cobblestones and watching the last drop of her innocence leaving her. She blinked. And then she saw it. In front and on top of her was the perfect picture of evil.

CHAPTER 1

The sound of Jo's voice echoing through the intercom sent Ciaran and Madeline charging up the stairs. They stormed into Tadgh's room, finding him lying flat on the floor, unconscious.

Ciaran took Tadgh's pulse. *Steady*, he mused. His brother was clinically alive and well.

But something was missing inside Tadgh. Something profound. Fundamental. Something that, as a scientist, he didn't care to speak of or even theorize.

Tadgh's soul is gone.

Ciaran shook his head. He couldn't believe he'd let that thought cross his mind. He had no idea how to explain this. Fear clawed at him.

He could cure his little brother of any earthly problem that could be scientifically explained. He had even manufactured the perfect level of sugar in Tadgh's blood—a minor issue Tadgh had when he was a kid.

Ciaran could even help with anything physiological or emotional his little brother might encounter. But the only thing he couldn't help Tadgh with was his mind.

That was the most scientific he could make it. Calling it *the mind.*

When it came to something as metaphysical as a soul, Ciaran didn't even know where to begin.

"How could this happen? One minute we were talking, and the next, he fell to the carpet!" Jo exclaimed.

"He's all right, Jo."

"He doesn't look all right, Ciaran. Is he traveling into another dimension like you did the day before yesterday?"

Ciaran shook his head. "Let's put him on the bed."

Madeline nodded. As soon as she grabbed Tadgh's arm to help, she yelped and released it. A tear rolled down her face.

"What is it, Madeline?" Ciaran asked.

Madeline's eyes were glazed for a short moment, and then they became clear again. "He saw Kyle Wolf. But not via his own eyes," she whispered.

"So whose eyes did he see the monster through?" Ciaran muttered, more to himself than to Madeline. It a rhetorical question. He didn't think Madeline knew the answer. But he had a feeling someone did. Ciaran looked at Jo.

The blood drained from Jo's face. "The eyes of the victim. He could see their emotion and the monster's emotion. He saw Kyle's satisfaction when he ripped the innocence out of someone. Like he once did to me," Jo spoke under her breath.

Ciaran grabbed Madeline's cold, shaky hands. "Sit down, will you?" He nudged her down onto a chair.

"It's horrible." A tear rolled down Madeline's face.

"Let it calm down. It will pass." He kissed her lightly. "Okay?" he asked. She nodded.

On the floor, Tadgh stirred, and his eyes fluttered and opened. Ciaran darted over. Tadgh's eyes were distant, as if he hadn't yet come back to reality. Then in a brief second, Ciaran knew his brother was back.

"Tadgh, you passed out. You remember anything?" Ciaran reached his hand out to pull him up.

Tadgh glanced around the room. He paused at Jo's face. Then his eyes hardened. The darkness in his brother's eyes worried Ciaran. "You can see emotion since you stupidly injected the poison into your body, but it shouldn't force you to *connect* with Kyle."

"No way am I connected with that monster. I don't have a choice here. I see what I see," Tadgh muttered. "Fuck this!" Tadgh kicked the chair, the table, and another piece of furniture as he moved across the room. Ciaran let him go for a couple of minutes then tackled him to the floor.

"Let go of me." Tadgh shoved Ciaran off and stood up.

"Do I have to assign security and keep you chained up, Tadgh? We're going to Australia tomorrow . . ."

"I'm going with you," Tadgh snarled.

"Give me a very good reason to allow that, Tadgh."

"I need to kill the fucking bastard."

"What did you see?"

"Can't tell you. And there's nothing you can do."

"You can't be sure of that," Ciaran countered.

Tadgh stared at Ciaran and said nothing more.

"Very well, you will stay here. I'll assign security and take away all of your access to transport." Ciaran strode toward the door of the room.

Tadgh darted after him and grabbed for Ciaran's shoulder. The momentum of Tadgh's hand pushed Ciaran, shoving him forward. "Don't be ridiculous, Ciaran. I can help you."

Entering the reception room at the end of the corridor, Ciaran turned around. "I said no. You and Jo stay here. I can't take care of you in Australia."

"Let me put this another way, big brother. How can you be so sure Kyle wouldn't try to kill *you* in Australia?" Tadgh cocked an eyebrow in challenge. "I need to go with you."

"Then tell me what you just saw."

"Kyle was doing what he did to Jo to another girl in London," Tadgh said and glanced at Jo.

"How did you see it? I could feel the vibration of Kyle's energy when I touched your arm," Madeline said.

Tadgh shook his head. "I didn't see much. Just got a glimpse of objects and shapes, and I heard some sounds. The shapes and sounds translate into emotion. That's what I feel. I extrapolate the action that cause the emotion and the owner of the emotions afterward."

Tadgh flopped into a reading chair and closed his eyes.

"And you did all that in a few minutes?" Jo asked.

"He's a walking, talking computer, Jo," Ciaran said.

"I can tell if Kyle is coming when he's miles away. Like now. He's in London. I can't tell the precise location. But if he takes any action on anyone, I can tell from miles away," Tadgh said.

"I can't risk him controlling you. Madeline and Jo saw that happen," Ciaran explained.

"Madeline knocked me out way before they could even tell if I was able to resist Kyle."

Ciaran looked at Madeline. She nodded to confirm what Tadgh had just said.

Tadgh grunted and held his head.

"I'll have to knock you out, Tadgh," Ciaran said.

Tadgh gestured for Ciaran to stay away. "It wasn't Kyle. It's the girl . . ." he grunted again and looked as if he was in excruciating pain. Ciaran approached.

"No, no. I can take this." Tadgh held his head and closed his eyes. After a while, he opened his eyes and looked at Ciaran. He was as white as a ghost.

"Turn on the news," Tadgh said numbly.

Ciaran turned on their private channel. As the latest news flashed, the blood drained from all of their faces.

CHAPTER 2

Kyle smiled to himself. He stood right in front of the small pub where his latest prey was doing whatever he made her do. He frowned. He had to be careful. He needed quite a few more innocent souls before he could crash the Daimon Gate opening in Australia. There was no room for error.

The attempt tonight had been a success, which pleased him a great deal. An eighteen-year-old girl in a dark alley. A weak-willed soul—and to his delight—a virtuous one.

Kyle chuckled and focused his gaze through the pub's small window to enjoy his victory. Nobody could see him unless he allowed them to. He was invisible to the naked eye. Yet the damage he did to the humans was quite visible.

He could stand right inside the pub, and all would be oblivious to his existence. He would probably enjoy the smoky ambiance where the humans congregated and tried to give one another lung cancer. The stench of fresh blood was pleasant to him. And he would certainly like the sound of metal and glass cutting into flesh. His senses had become a lot more acute these days.

But no. He didn't want to mix with humans. He was once a Eudaizian, a citizen of a beautiful universe in which he was born—and which he still longed for. He would forever be a Eudaizian in his heart, even though they had exiled him and stripped him of all his rights.

Well, he would take all of those rights back.

Soon.

Chaos in the pub. Screams. Cries. Crashes. Blood splattered onto the windows. People shoved at the heavy oak door and stormed outside.

The young girl grabbed a knife, possibly a steak knife, and slaughtered everyone in her way. She was especially interested in those that holding balloons and banners for the surprise birthday party.

He had heard that thought screaming in the girl's head when he had raped her soul. After thirty-three years living on this hell hole called Earth, he had learned what birthdays meant to humans. He still couldn't understand why they celebrated their earthly existence when the soul meant so much more than the body.

Kyle shook his head. Anyway, who cared?

He didn't care how many people the girl was killing in the pub. Those casualties didn't count on his score card. The innocent soul of the girl counted, though. She counted as one.

Kyle sighed. He needed more than that. So he needed the girl to hurry up, kill someone, and then kill herself. That was the final tick in the box to ensure that tonight was a success.

Police sirens echoed in the distance. He should help the girl before people talked her out of the final step, the last step in being his score.

Kyle closed his eyes. When he opened them, the girl appeared on the roof of the building. She looked down as if scared. Tears streamed down her face. Her hair flew and tangled in the winter wind. She held onto the chimney.

"Come on, darling. Jump. I'll catch your soul," Kyle mumbled to himself.

The girl started to cry, and her legs began to wobble. She hung on tightly and leaned on the chimney so that her knees wouldn't buckle.

"It's all right. It won't be bad at all. Come on, sweetheart. I'll take you to heaven. Come to me," Kyle whispered.

The girl cried out loud. Kyle knew too well that she was at the extreme of her conflicting emotions. He couldn't let her give in to her survival instinct or his attempt would be ruined. He couldn't let the girl do the opposite of what he wanted her to do.

Kyle Wolf had never been defeated in that way.

He closed his eyes and chanted an ancient spell. This was his last resource. He'd never had to rely on magic before. Ever. Magic was what ruined his Master. But he had no choice now. He cast the spell.

And in no time, the girl's body landed in front of the cameraman of the news crew who had just arrived on the scene.

Kyle smiled. *Success*. He turned around to hunt for a few more souls.

CHAPTER 3

Ciaran's little hands gripped the ledge outside his room's window tightly, and he climbed out to the roof. There was no way he was going to be grounded in his room for a week. He was four, and he was entitled to make a case with his father. If Father listened.

Father always encouraged Tadgh to talk. And that was fair enough because his brother was just learning to talk. But Ciaran knew he was able to speak at a level beyond his age. If it wasn't true, would Father have given him books in philosophy last year?

So why had Father just grounded him this time without even listening to his reasons?

Those wild dogs had attacked and killed Dew, his German shepherd. What was wrong with a little retaliation?

And he didn't do much damage or hurt anyone. He had mixed the explosive, and he'd tested it on the statue of the Goddess of Kindness in the garden. It was only a statue! And he didn't blow up the whole thing . . . just the head.

So why was father so upset?

Ciaran looked down the slope of the roof. It was quite steep. But that was all right. He had strong grip.

He scooted his bare little feet along the roof tiles, carefully lowered himself down to the gutter, and then dropped down to the ground. He pulled out the slippers he had folded into the pockets of his pajamas, put them on, and strode toward the back garden.

Soon he stood at the hill at the back of Mon Ciel.

The dark hill was covered with bushes, ancient trees, and numerous paths that led to places in the woods where Father would never let him go. Ciaran wasn't afraid of the dark—or anything else for that matter. He was willing to explore and learn.

What was wrong with Father lately?

He missed Dew. Until his little brother had grown up and could speak a bit more, Dew had been his only friend. He looked up the hill to where the wild dogs had killed his dog, and he ground his teeth.

He hated those dogs.

He knew his father wouldn't approve of such strong emotion. A kid his age wasn't supposed to feel hatred—or even know what it meant.

But he really missed Dew. A tear rolled down his face. And that was what he couldn't allow.

He was four.

He was a big brother.

And he would not cry.

The fury had blasted at him then for the first time. He didn't know where it had come from, but he knew he was furious. His temperature increased. His blood boiled. His head felt as if it was going to explode.

The next thing he knew, blades of something hit the forest in front of him with incredible force. Trees were trimmed down to the roots. Dirt, grass, and rocks flew into the air as the gigantic blades hit the ground, chopping everything in their path.

The blades spun and flew around like gigantic fans from alien spaceships. In seconds, they had carved the hill down to its bare rock bed. He was sure that all the ancient trees and animals in the little forest had been exterminated.

Ciaran fell on his backside. He knew the blades had come from his mind. They were a tangible form of his fury. They came from his thoughts of killing.

In front of him now was the scene of a war zone.

Now he understood why his father had worked so hard to teach him to control his temper. Why his father had tried everything in his power to stop any trace of violence in his thought processes.

His father had to talk him out of violence without being able to give examples or demonstrations of the consequences if he did otherwise. Because *this* was a live demonstration of what could happen. If there had been anyone in the forest during that time, their lives were lost. He hoped there had been no one lurking in the bushes in the middle of this winter night.

But he would never know.

Another tear fell onto his cheek. Now he was upset because he wasn't allowed to be upset anymore. He wondered what would happen if he cried.

He dare not try. He didn't even want to think about it.

Ciaran went quietly home and climbed back into his room.

"Ciaran!" Madeline called him from behind, snapping him back to reality. He was staring at the very window that he had climbed out on his way to experience the power of his fury for the first time.

He turned around and smiled at her.

"What are you doing here?" she asked.

"This was my room when I was a kid."

"Oh . . ." Madeline looked around. Then she embraced him. It embarrassed him how much he had grown to crave her embraces. He held her in his arms and looked out the window.

When they had seen the news and realized Kyle had possessed the girl in London and had told her to kill herself and the others, Madeline had called Kyle a monster. What would she think if she knew his mind had a destructive power that made Kyle's ability look like child's play? What she would think of him if she knew he could kill—and did kill—with just a thought?

He kissed the dimple of her left cheek, then he looked into her eyes. "I need to tell you something."

CHAPTER 4

Madeline assumed that Australia had changed a lot in ten years. She had. She was a new person, and she had a new life. Now she was going back to Australia to start another life—a life in Eudaiz. Who would have thought?

New York certainly had drifted into a far distant past.

They were greeted by a wave of skin-blistering heat as soon as they hit the tarmac at Melbourne's Tullamarine airport. They had departed England's bitter winter and were now hit by Australia's sweltering heat. These were the two extremes of weather on Earth, and Madeline wondered what it would be like in Eudaiz, another universe.

Thanks to the organization of Ciaran's staff, they were scooped into a luxurious air-conditioned car. She did not care which car they used, but she definitely needed a buffer for her sensitive skin to adjust to the temperature difference.

After much discussion, Ciaran had agreed that Tadgh and Jo could come along, with a list of terms and conditions that would take a lifetime to enumerate. In a nutshell, if Tadgh so much as sneezed wrong, Ciaran would send him back to England in a heartbeat.

As much as Madeline thought Tadgh was immature and impatient, she knew he would go to any lengths when it came to Ciaran's welfare. The LeBlanc brothers were genuinely a pack.

It didn't shock her at all when Ciaran told her about what his mind could do. That it could kill. That Ciaran could cause a massacre with a blade he kept locked in his mind.

There had to be a very good reason he was the chosen one for the most important Sciphil position in Eudaiz.

She knew this was just the beginning. She only hoped he was ready to take on the responsibilities.

Late in the afternoon, after several phone calls back and forth between Jo and Zach, they drove out to meet him at Tropical Tunes, the hub of Zach's band. As a frequent traveler, Tadgh knew his way around Melbourne, so he took the wheel.

Madeline glanced at the trendy modern restaurant bar when they arrived.

"You thought it would be different?" Jo asked Madeline.

"It sounded like a Hawaiian pizza place." Madeline chuckled.

A voice came from the corner of the empty restaurant. "You almost got it right. The tropical part is the cuisine, and Hawaiian pizza *is* on the menu. We handle the music part, and there's nothing tropical at all about our music."

A young man approached. "You must be Zach's friends. He told me to wait for you. He'll be here soon. We're not open yet, so the restaurant is yours."

He looked at Jo. "This must be Jo. I'm Peter." Peter bent his lanky body down to kiss Jo's cheek. "Your picture didn't do you any justice."

Jo narrowed her eyes. "What picture?"

"Ah, your avatar. I'm a beginner. Learning the games, you know. Zach taught me a lot. But I'm in no way near a level where I could play with you."

Jo nodded. "Hologame fan. Don't worry. You'll get there. You've got a good mentor. This is Madeline, Tadgh, and Ciaran. We just came from—"

"England right? Zach told me. I want to visit there some day."

"I'll be happy to host you when you visit," Ciaran said.

Peter looked at him. "What kind of music do you play?"

"I'm not a musician." Ciaran smiled. Madeline understood where Peter's assumption had come from. Ciaran looked the type.

"Can I get you something to drink?" Peter asked. His eyes didn't leave Jo. Tadgh stepped forward, blocking Peter's view of her.

"A beer would be good. It's a hot day," Tadgh said.

"Sure," Peter said and scurried away.

Ciaran raised an eyebrow at his brother. "Since when do you drink beer?"

"I'm not as predictable as you might think."

A motorbike zoomed in and parked right in front of the restaurant.

And in walked Zach Flynn. He took his helmet off, revealing his easy style of brown hair, an unshaven face, and killer eyes. He wore a leather jacket and jeans that sheathed long, well-toned legs and a backside that constantly made his groupies wild. Zach had aged a bit in ten years, but time had definitely worked in his favor, Madeline observed.

Jo leaped out of the chair next to Tadgh and gave Zach a bear hug. Zach picked her up and spun her around. "It's so good to see you," Zach said.

He put Jo down and walked toward Madeline. "Madeline, I don't have the words to describe how beautiful you look." He kissed her cheek, and Madeline smiled.

"I can help in that regard." Ciaran reached his hand out for a handshake.

"You must be Ciaran." Zach gave Ciaran's hand an earnest shake. "White Knight. It's an honor to meet you."

Ciaran glanced at Jo.

"I figured it out myself." Zach smiled. "Any real hologame player would know about you, Ciaran."

Ciaran nodded.

Zach and Tadgh gave each other measured looks while they exchanged handshakes.

Peter entered the room with a tray of beers.

Zach glanced at the beer and raised an eyebrow at Peter. "You're going to make the ladies drink out of a bottle? And that's Victorian Bitter that you're serving!"

"I don't mind." Jo grabbed a bottle. Everyone did the same while Peter scratched his head.

Zach excused himself. He gave Peter some instructions and sent him away. He then returned to the table and picked up his beer.

"Sorry. There's an audition for a guitarist tonight. The band has to move on while I'm away."

"What did you tell people about your trip?" Tadgh asked.

Zach shook his head. Madeline caught a flash of reluctance and exhaustion from him. "Told them I'd be traveling." Zach leaned back in his chair. His eyes were distant and cold.

"Zach, does that mean your friends and family know nothing about this trip?" Madeline asked.

Zach shrugged. "I don't know what to tell them."

"You've got to be kidding me!" Tadgh exclaimed. "You know this is important. People could get killed even before entering the gate. If you don't care about your own life, that's fine. But Ciaran and Madeline have to go through with this—

"I might not go . . ."

"What the fuck!" Tadgh exclaimed.

"I used to have that option," Zach snarled.

"Keep your voices down!" Ciaran warned. "Is there somewhere we can talk without an audience?"

Zach stood up and nodded toward the stairs. Then he strode away.

CHAPTER 5

Before following Zach upstairs, Madeline pulled at Ciaran's elbow to hold him back. "Ciaran, Zach and Jo used to be together. It was a very long time ago. I think they're fine now. He's moved on, has a girlfriend—last time I heard, they were engaged. He has a career, a large family, and a life here."

Ciaran pinched lightly at her dimple and smiled. "You're saying he has a life and has a lot to lose."

Madeline smiled.

"I'll be gentle with him," Ciaran said and winked at her.

When Ciaran and Madeline got upstairs, Zach had cleared the room and made sure no staff was lurking around.

The room felt warm and welcoming. Judging by the musical instruments scattered on the floor, Madeline bet Zach used this as a studio to teach music.

Zach sat down on a high stool next to a counter. "Look, I don't know what to tell my family, okay? Originally, it was just the opening of a gate for me, which shouldn't be a big deal. Ayana told me that being the successor of Sciphil Two will not be difficult, and I'll have all the flexibility to go back and forth like Pete Chandler."

"So what changed?" Madeline asked.

"Well, you two are going to tailgate me . . ."

"Tailgating?" Tadgh snorted.

"Yeah, I thought the same. No big deal. But it's different with Ciaran because he's not just a Sciphil. He's a *King* Sciphil. His route will be different and more difficult."

"You received training, and you know what's involved?" Ciaran asked.

Zach nodded. "Hell yeah. For other Sciphils, it's like multilevel hologames—not easy, but doable. Yours is a nasty combo."

"Like what?" Ciaran asked.

"Well, Ayana was saying something about a nine-by-nine dimensional scenario, whatever that means."

"A matrix. That means you won't know what's coming at you," Tadgh mumbled.

"I don't think so. There should be options for normal routes and for the King Sciphils. The selection of scenarios should be monitored based on the level of difficulty. It shouldn't be random. If there's some logic to it, then we can work out a solution," Ciaran said.

"It was hard enough handling the deal by myself. I just found out about your tailgating a few days ago. Haven't had any other conversations with Ayana, and haven't had any further training or information about what the fuck I am getting myself into."

Zach stood up and went to a small bar at the corner of the room. He spoke from the bar. "I'm not scared or anything. But I don't want to go in without knowing if I have a chance to come back to my family. It's not like we're going to war, and I can pretend to be patriotic. I don't even know whose war we're fighting here! Some aliens—"

"They're people just like us, Zach," Ciaran said. "They might have a different makeup, and live in a different universe, but they face life and death just like us. If you expand the boundary of your country, where you claim your patriotism, to the boundaries of the Earth, the universe, and the multiverse, then you can see that people are ultimately the same, and you are protecting them against evil."

"Look Ciaran, I have no intention of getting philosophical here. I'm no hero. I'm just a guy. I play guitar, I teach music, and I have a band. That's all I ever wanted."

"Why did you agree to it in the first place?" Madeline asked.

Zach stared at Madeline. "I can't tell you."

"If you think . . ." Madeline trailed off when Peter raced into the room.

"Sorry to interrupt. The restaurant is opening now, and also the guy is coming for the audition . . ."

"What guy?" Zach asked.

"The audition. The guitarist, Zach."

"Oh, okay. Fine. John, isn't it?" Zach shook his head.

"Yeah, John. Mate, he needs a stage name. John Smith isn't gonna work," Peter said, laughing.

"Can we wait until we actually hire him to think of his stage name?"

"Right, that's right." Peter scratched his head and walked away while Zach rolled his eyes.

Zach turned around. "I might have to go downstairs to watch this audition—"

"Your decision to go through the gate might be pending," Ciaran cut in.

"No, it's not. The deal was sealed." Zach showed the thumbprint on his right arm.

Ciaran sat down on a high stool next to a music stand. He shook his head. "Madeline and I are committed to go through the gate. We have our reasons. If you were so unsure, why did you agree?"

Zach gazed hard at Ciaran. "As I said, I can't tell you. I let you tailgate me. That's it. I promised, and I will go through with it."

"I'm afraid it won't be that simple. We might have a gate-crasher. I need to know all that's necessary to deal with it."

Zach arched an eyebrow. "Who?"

"His name is Kyle Wolf. He's an exiled Sciphil and a mind-bender," Ciaran said.

Zach looked at Madeline. She could see thousands of questions in his eyes.

"Why'd you call him a mind-bender?" Zach asked.

"In theory, he sends mind-wave signals to control people's thought processes and behaviors," Ciaran said.

Zach arched an eyebrow. "And you can't tell he's doing it by looking at him?"

"He controls the projection of his visibility in people's mind. Nobody can see him unless he wants them to. When he controls a person, it looks as though the person is possessed," Ciaran explained.

"This is ridiculous. Total bullshit. You can't even see the guy . . ."

An eardrum-bursting guitar sound echoed up from downstairs.

"Oh, fuck me. If they let this guy play, the club will have no customers left," Zach snarled and strode toward the stairs to go down to the club.

Madeline quickly stepped in front of him. "Zach, if you're scared, that's fine. I'm scared, too. But if you think we don't understand what happened ten years ago in the bush, then you're wrong. We know."

Zach turned around. He pointed at Ciaran, Tadgh, and Jo. "They all know?"

"Yes."

Zach shook his head. "It's not possible. You don't know half of it, Madeline. I killed the old man. Okay? Are you happy now? " He paused then said, "I have to go stop that fucking noise."

Zach pushed toward the stairs. The sound of the guitar surged and swelled, accompanied by a drum that sounded like someone was beating on an empty laundry bucket.

Madeline stopped Zach. He nudged her aside.

As quick as a cat, Ciaran darted toward Zach, grabbed him from behind, and spun him against the far wall.

"Keep your hands off her," Ciaran growled.

Zach shoved Ciaran.

"You don't know what I can do to you, Ciaran."

"Try me!"

Ciaran and Zach glared menacingly at each other.

CHAPTER 6

A mixture of strange noises echoed up from the room downstairs. Zach heard the noise, but he didn't take his eyes off Ciaran. Ciaran held his gaze as well. They looked as if they were trying to shoot each other with their stares.

Madeline approached Ciaran. He gestured for her to stay away. His eyes didn't leave Zach for a second.

The two held their stances and remained locked in their staring competition for a few moments.

Zach broke the silence. "I have to go," he snarled.

"You are not going anywhere until we talk things out. We only have one day before the gate opening."

"That's your problem. I'm letting you go through my gate. What else do you want from me?"

"Your full cooperation. I need all relevant information."

Zach sneered. "Now that's a king's order from someone who hasn't even made it to the throne yet."

The drum and the guitar below kept pounding away. Zach clenched his teeth then said, "Get out of my way, or you'll regret it."

"Do your best."

Ciaran and Zach stared at each other once again, their eyes intense. Ciaran stepped forward. Zach staggered back a step then held his stance.

A drop of blood trickled from Zach's nose. Then another. Then the same happened to Ciaran.

Zach grunted and slumped to the floor, more blood trickling from his nose.

The sound of the guitar downstairs had stopped, and sounds of chaos took its place.

Zach sat on the floor, leaning against the wall. Jo checked on him.

Madeline gave Ciaran a handkerchief for his bleeding nose. When she touched his hand, it was as cold as ice. Ciaran moved toward the high music stool and sat down.

Peter thumped up the stairs and stormed into the room, puffing. "John passed out for no reason. His nose and ears are bleeding . . ." His voice trailed off when he saw Zach. "Jesus Christ. Did John sound that bad?"

Tadgh grabbed Peter and turned him toward the stairs. "No, no, it was fine. We had a slight disagreement up here. Zach is just fine. Nothing to do with what happened downstairs. Off you go. Get John a doctor." Tadgh pushed Peter outside the room and slammed the door closed.

Zach stood up. He went over to sit opposite Ciaran.

Madeline saw a coffee jug on a table in the corner of the room.

"Can I get you some coffee?" she asked.

"Yes, please," Ciaran said.

"No, thanks. I prefer something stronger, but I'll get it later," Zach told her.

Jo and Tadgh went to the table to get the coffee.

Madeline brought a cup to Ciaran. She touched his hands to see if they were still cold and was pleased to feel their warmth had returned.

"Zach, when did you know you were a sound-bender?" Ciaran asked.

"Since longer than I can remember."

"Your family doesn't know, I guess?"

Zach shook his head. "No point advertising the fact that I'm a freak show."

"In Eudaiz, they'd call it a talent. That's why Ayana recruited you. Sound-bending seems to be her department. You should see what she did to Madeline."

"What?"

"Don't worry about it, Zach. It's not important," Madeline said.

"Did you use your sound-bending talent to kill the man in the bush?" Ciaran asked.

Zach grabbed his head and messed his hair up. He looked at Ciaran. Zach looked so tired, Madeline thought.

"I don't label my ability. Call it whatever you want, but I definitely wouldn't call it a talent. I can make a sound in my head and send that sound to anyone's head. Most of the time, it just messes people up."

"Like the way you shut the guitarist up?" Tadgh asked.

Zach nodded. "I don't have total control of it. And it doesn't work the same on everyone. When

42

I've tried it on someone strong, the sound has bounced back to me. Usually harder."

"You tried it on Ciaran. How did it feel?" Tadgh asked.

Zach looked at Tadgh and shrugged.

Tadgh waved his finger at Zach. "Don't you even think about trying it out on me. I won't stand and take it like Ciaran did. I'd kick your ass before you even got a chance to send out a sound wave."

"Does it kill, Zach?" Jo asked.

Zach looked at Jo, devastated. Jo embraced him. "I'm sorry. You just wanted to save me. I was in bad shape."

Zach held Jo and buried his head in her shoulder.

In the corner of the room, Tadgh shifted.

"I helped kill that man, too, Zach. Don't take all the responsibility yourself," Madeline said.

Zach looked up at everyone. "The guy was evil. He had that look the very minute he laid eyes on Jo. I was pissed off. I thought I'd mess with his head. Make him go crazy. The next thing I knew, he went crazy enough to kill his wife and his kids. Then I killed him and set the house on fire."

Zach didn't realize a tear had trickled down his face.

"It wasn't you, Zach. Kyle was there. He was controlling the man. He made him kill his family," Madeline said.

Zach shook his head. "I did it, and I've lived with it for ten years. There was no mind-bender or whatever in the bush. It was only me—and a curse you call a talent—that killed those people. Ayana knew that. She didn't blackmail me. She just offered me a chance to save a lot of people and do something good . . . There, I've said it. Do whatever you want with me."

"A chance for redemption, and she got you," Ciaran muttered.

"Redemption is too fancy a word for me."

The phone in the corner of the room rang a few times and went to voice mail. A female voice spoke. "Zach, it's Chloe. Where are you? I've been calling you for the last ten minutes. When you get this message, call me back. It's Riko—she's in your apartment . . ."

Zach cursed and snatched the phone. "I'm here . . ."

Zach listened and then put down the phone. "Sorry, guys, gotta go," he said while running toward the door.

CHAPTER 7

Later, in the car, Ciaran was driving and glancing around at the same time. They had lost Zach. Tadgh concentrated to see if he could channel Riko the way he had connected to the young girl in London. But nothing came to his mind.

"Any info, Tadgh?" Ciaran asked.

"Nothing."

"Madeline, any direction?" Ciaran asked.

Madeline closed her eyes. They speculated that whatever had happened with whomever Zach had been talking to on the phone was the result of Kyle Wolf's interference. Although they had lost Zach in traffic, they followed Madeline's instinct of where Kyle would be.

"Left. On the left," Madeline said.

Without hesitation, Ciaran turned abruptly onto the street to the left.

"It's a one-way street, and you're going the wrong way, Ciaran!" Tadgh yelled from the back seat.

Ciaran ignored both him and the honks and rude gestures from the other drivers and made his way to where he could turn onto the next street and drive the right way.

"It's here," Madeline said. "The reeks of Kyle Wolf."

Tadgh glanced at the scene. It was a quiet street with several apartment complexes. They parked the car and headed toward the closest building. He still couldn't feel Riko or Kyle. He scolded himself. What was wrong with his newfound talent?

They heard Zach's voice. "Come on, Riko. Come down. You don't want to do this."

They went around the corner of the building and saw Zach standing in a small courtyard looking up to level four. A young Asian girl sat on the ledge outside the balcony railing. Her legs dangled, her long hair flowed in the wind, and her eyes darkened. She stared down at Zach but said nothing. Her face was completely void of expression.

On the other side of the balcony railing was a tall and stunning blonde girl. She stood there, phone in hand, shaking. Madeline guessed she must be Chloe.

Zach paid no attention to the incoming people. He focused on Riko.

"Shouldn't you call the police?" Tadgh asked.

"She does this every second week. She won't jump."

Ciaran lowered his voice. "She'll jump this time, Zach. And the blood will be on your hands if you don't do what I say."

"What?" Sweat trickled down Zach's forehead.

"I told you. It's Kyle Wolf. He controls people's minds. But he can only do it to one person at a time. So do what I say," Ciaran said.

Tadgh stared at the girl, trying to probe her emotions. Nothing. He couldn't see or feel anything, but a cold chill ran up and down his spine.

"I'll go up," Tadgh said and charged toward the back entrance. Jo and Madeline went around the back and up the stairs.

Before picking the lock of the apartment, Tadgh signaled Ciaran's phone. Receiving the signal, Ciaran said, "Now, send your sound wave to Riko."

Zach shifted, then began.

The sound hit, and Riko lifted her chin up. She blinked her eyes.

Zach staggered back. Blood trickled from his nose.

"The sound bounced back to you because it hit Kyle. He's strong, Zach. Can you hold?" Ciaran asked while grabbing at Zach and supporting him from the back. Zach nodded and fixed his stance.

Tadgh, Jo, and Madeline broke into the apartment and hurried toward the balcony.

Riko looked around, looked down, and started crying. She shook, stood up, and began to climb back over the railing.

Chloe yelled at Riko. "Jump! You were supposed to jump!" Chloe pushed at Riko while Riko was on top of the railing. Riko cried and clung to the railing as tightly as she could.

Chloe grunted out the words again. "Jump! I told you to jump!"

On the ground, Ciaran said, "He's got Chloe now. Send the sound to her."

From the apartment, Tadgh grabbed Chloe, pulling her inside while she kicked and screamed.

Jo helped Riko climb over the railing and get safely onto the balcony.

Madeline ran to the kitchen and grabbed a knife. She filled a bucket she found in the corner with water.

In the living room, Chloe still kicked and screamed like a madwoman. Tadgh held her, but he had the feeling he would not be able to hang on for long. Her strength was incredible. It was almost supernatural.

On the ground, Zach sent more sound signals. Both his nose and his ears were bleeding now.

Jo ran to the balcony and called out, "Tadgh's got her now. It's okay."

Zach stopped the signal and slumped to the ground.

"You think I got him?" Zach asked.

Ciaran shook his head. "Don't know. Can you get up there?"

Zach nodded. They ran up the stairs.

Inside the apartment, Madeline splashed water everywhere. Jo grabbed a knife, too. She pushed Riko into a corner and kept an eye on her in case she was taken over again. Jo focused on where Madeline sprayed the water. If she saw any sign of the beast, Jo swore to God that she would stab it until it was nothing but pulp.

Chloe grew stronger by the second. She shrugged off Tadgh.

Ciaran and Zach stormed into the apartment.

Chloe jumped on top of the table.

As soon as Tadgh lost Chloe, he felt a strange sensation at the back of his neck. He heard something echo in his head. His vision blurred. He felt an urge to act on something. He felt as if he was waiting for an order.

Tadgh closed his eyes and shook his head. He knew what was happening.

He saw Chloe standing on the table. She leaped as though she could fly, aiming straight for the glass coffee table.

Tadgh heard a clear voice in his head. "Step aside. Let the bitch fall." Tadgh knew he had to act against the voice. He focused.

There was a very strong sensation urging him to obey and do what the voice had said. Tadgh grunted. The voice was telling him to step aside. Tadgh clenched his teeth, rushed toward the table, and caught Chloe mid-flight.

They both fell onto the glass coffee table with Chloe on top of Tadgh.

Tadgh's vision cleared. The voice was no longer in his head. There was no more sensation, but he felt a searing pain on his back.

He saw Madeline and Jo leap to a corner and stab at something.

There was a sound like a roar.

Then he saw Ciaran. Ciaran said something. Tadgh could have responded, but for some reason, he thought he would be better off shutting his mind down and letting go.

Tadgh passed out on the floor in a pool of his own blood.

CHAPTER 8

Kyle clung to the ledge of the hospital's window and looked inside. He was sure the humans couldn't see him. But his hands were still shaky, and he was still in shock from the attack on him at the apartment. He wasn't sure about much of anything now.

Madeline and Jo, those bitches! The LeBlanc boys. The Australian musician. I'll kill you all! Kyle clenched his teeth. He had found the weak link in the group—Tadgh. Kyle smiled as he peeked into the room. He could get into Tadgh's mind. Tadgh couldn't guard his mind the way the others could, but Kyle knew he had to be careful because Tadgh had an extremely strong will.

Kyle crawled through the window.

"Damn!" He sensed Madeline at the end of the corridor. She could sense him. He couldn't fight yet. He climbed back out and fled.

***

Tadgh opened his eyes in an emergency room to Jo throwing herself at him. She hugged him and buried her face in his neck. She stayed like that for a long time but said nothing.

"I've had quite a few women propelling themselves at me in a short period of time. Is this an Australian thing?"

Jo sat up. Her big green eyes filled with tears.

"Oh, no. Don't cry, beautiful. This is just a little scratch."

Jo could not keep those big tears from rolling down her face.

"If a little scratch incapacitated you for a few hours, it's no wonder Ciaran considered sending you home."

"What?" Tadgh winced with the pain.

Zach and Chloe walked in. Chloe had a few cuts and bruises which had been tended to. She approached Tadgh's bed.

"Zach told me you took the brunt of the table for me. Thank you. I'm so sorry. I can't remember a thing."

Zach stood behind Chloe. He looked at Tadgh and shook his head, telling him silently not to say anything to Chloe.

"I can handle a glass table, but I can't handle tears from those green eyes. Could you help me stop them?" Tadgh nodded at Jo.

Jo wiped at her face.

"Why don't you both go outside for some fresh air? Don't go too far, though," Zach said.

Chloe nodded and took Jo out of the room.

"How are you doing, really?" Zach asked.

"It hurts like a bitch." Tadgh winced again.

"You've lost some blood. Your brother was royally pissed."

"Why? It's not as though I *wanted* to fall on the table."

"I don't know. He's pissed at something. Maybe it's not you. Maybe he's pissed at that fucking dickhead, Kyle Wolf."

"Well, let him be mad," Tadgh mumbled.

"The beast really got to Chloe, man. She can't remember a thing. She was really out of control."

Tadgh rolled his eyes. "Tell me about it."

"I guess it's true what Ciaran said about the mind-bender. He messed up the man in the bush and made him kill his family. It wasn't me at all."

"So now you're not going through the gate?"

"Yeah, I will. I promised. And there are . . ."

Ciaran and Madeline entered the room.

"How are you doing, Tadgh?" Madeline asked.

"I've been better. Some pretty intense stabbing you and Jo did at the apartment." Tadgh grinned.

"Yeah, I can do a lot of damage. Where's Jo?" Madeline asked.

"Out with Chloe," Zach said.

Ciaran stood still and said nothing.

"I've got to take Chloe home." Zach glanced outside to ensure that Chloe had not come back. "Here's the thing. I agreed to go through the gate partly to redeem myself from what happened in the bush but mainly because of what happened a few weeks ago."

Zach looked toward the door again and saw no sign of Chloe.

He continued, "I went back to the bush to visit the site again to remind myself of what I did . . ."

Madeline shook her head.

"And when I came back, there was a strange aura following me. All hell broke loose from there. Spooky stuff like voodoo and possession occurred. People died. *I* almost died. The girl you saw, Riko, she was one of the survivors."

"You think it was Kyle?" Tadgh asked.

"Before, no. My friend, Dan, called it the Zodiac Shifter because Kyle attacked people based on their zodiac signs. Dan is into supernatural and paranormal stuff. I'm not. I thought the 'thing'— whatever it was—had done something similar to my sound-bending trick. I hadn't told anyone I'm a freak show, so I couldn't tell anyone about the mind-bending suspicion, either."

Ciaran nodded.

"Sciphil Nine approached me and told me if I agreed to be a Sciphil successor, I could help a lot of people, so I jumped at the chance. Pete referred only to what had happened in the bush," Zach continued.

"Ayana and Pete didn't know about Kyle going around killing innocent people based on the zodiac signs?" Ciaran asked.

"I don't think so. I wanted to kill the bastard, so I agreed."

Ciaran nodded. "That's fair enough."

"I couldn't make the connection. But I know now—after what happened today— that the bastard in the bush and the Zodiac Shifter could be the same guy and could be Kyle Wolf . . ." Zach said, trailing off when Chloe and Jo entered the room.

"We'll talk more tomorrow, Zach," Ciaran said.

Zach nodded and left the room to take Chloe home.

"I've made arrangements for some accommodations outside the city," Ciaran said.

"Thank God. This hospital bed is killing my backside." Tadgh sat up and winced with pain. Madeline helped him out of the bed.

"If you withhold any information from me, I'll send you home, Tadgh," Ciaran warned.

"Ciaran, not now, not here," Madeline told him.

"I don't know what you're talking about," Tadgh said.

"I know you, Tadgh. There's no chance you would have willingly copped the fall," Ciaran continued.

"Ciaran, let's go to our accommodations first."

Ciaran stopped talking and strode out of the room. Madeline knew that was the best way for him to handle a situation when he was steaming. They'd had a long discussion. Ciaran suspected Tadgh took the fall on purpose to avoid Kyle controlling him.

Ciaran suspected Tadgh was vulnerable to Kyle's attacks.

CHAPTER 9

The mansion was half an hour's drive from the city. It was imposing but homey. It surprised Madeline that the area became so rural after only a ten minutes' drive out of the city. But she had to admit she knew little about the rural concept. She shouldn't be calling an area rural based only on its lack of high-rises and traffic and the fact that she could hear animals. She knew for a fact that some people in New York had pet tigers in their apartments in the middle of the city. And New York was obviously not a jungle.

Ciaran had chosen to stay in Werribee because the LeBlancs had a lab nearby. He needed to make further arrangements for the trip the day after tomorrow.

Early in the morning, Madeline went out for a walk around the mansion. She knew Ciaran had been up and about for a while. But she wanted to give him a bit more time to do what he needed to do. He would find her when he needed her input.

Toward the back of the garden, she saw Tadgh sitting on a fence, smoking.

"First of all, I didn't know you smoked. Second, it's a huge fire hazard to smoke next to a barn."

Tadgh grinned and put out his cigarette. "A bad habit I developed from traveling a lot. Helps clear my head."

"Smoke and clarity really don't belong in the same sentence, Tadgh. But sometimes I prefer a muddy head so I don't have to think at all."

Tadgh laughed. "Muddy head! What a description."

"What do you need a clear head for? Anything I can help with?"

Tadgh shook his head. "Nah. I don't even know what I need. Better go inside to see what Ciaran is up to."

"How's your back?"

"Fine. Thanks."

Madeline gazed into Tadgh's eyes. "You can see people's emotions, Tadgh. I'm sure you can see Ciaran's gigantic concern about you being susceptible to Kyle's control. If that's the case, you have to tell us."

"So that he'll send me home?"

"Better than losing you to Kyle."

"I told you I'd kill the bastard, Madeline. I saw what he did to the girl in London. I saw what he did to Jo. He might be invisible, but he's not invincible. He's not human, but I think he has flesh and blood of some kind and can be hurt. Especially judging from the fact he roared like a pig when you stabbed him. So I just need time to think. I'll figure out how to kill him."

Madeline nodded. "All right. But if he gets into your head, I *will* knock you out."

"Deal." Tadgh smiled. "Your grandfather said Kyle was a Sciphil, and he was dealing with Black Rock. Is that right?"

"Yes. Something happened in Eudaiz. I think he somehow snatched me and ran to Earth. He was exiled. So he can't open the Daimon Gate and go back to Eudaiz himself. He has to tailgate us. But why kill people for their innocent souls?" Madeline asked.

Tadgh snorted. "Typical psychology of evil. I think it has to do with the Black Rock. Kyle betrayed Eudaiz for the Black Rock. He must have made some sort of deal—that he had to control and rape innocent souls. Some sort of a score."

"That's a scary thought. How did you figure that out?"

"Got it from my big brother. Ciaran uses the same principles to design evil guys in his hologames."

Madeline shook her head. "Sometimes real life is stranger than fiction. Unfortunately, Kyle is not a character in a game. . ." She trailed off. "Tadgh, what is it? What are you thinking about?"

"Huh?"

"You just had that faraway look on your face. You thought of something?"

Tadgh nodded. "I just put some things together. I might have something—"

Madeline gasped. "Jesus Christ."

"What is that?" Tadgh instinctively pushed Madeline behind him.

"Kyle. Run! Go inside, Tadgh!"

CHAPTER 10

Tadgh and Madeline stormed into the reception room and almost trampled Jo. The breakfast tray Jo was carrying flew through the air and fell to the floor. Coffee cups, a teapot, croissants, bread, plates, and other sundry items scattered on the floor.

"My breakfast is ruined! What a start to the day." Jo scowled. "What's wrong?" she asked.

Then she saw the look on Madeline's face.

"Kyle." Jo clenched her teeth and grabbed the butter knife from the floor. Tadgh grabbed her and held her back.

"Jo, that's a butter knife you've got. Do you really think you can kill a beast with that?" Tadgh asked.

"Would you prefer I use my fingernails?"

"I won't let you go out there," Tadgh said.

"Put that the other way around, pal. I won't let *you* go out there. Kyle can't get to me. But he can definitely get to you. So you're staying right here." Jo jabbed her finger at his shoulder.

Tadgh grabbed her arm. "Don't point your finger at me, young lady."

Jo mocked his British accent, "Oh, this lady is definitely pointing the finger at you!"

Ciaran walked into the room and saw the commotion. "What the heck is going on?"

"Kyle was out there. These two are fighting over who's going to go out there and take the hit. Don't worry, Ciaran. I'm not letting either one of them go," Madeline said dryly as she pointed to Jo and Tadgh.

"And how do you plan to fight Kyle, you two? What weapons are you going to use?" Ciaran asked.

"She's going to use a butter knife!" Tadgh snorted.

"Better than your fists. You could barely hold a woman in check last night," Jo ranted.

"I saved her life!" Tadgh raised his voice.

"Then who will save yours?" Jo squealed and threw the butter knife at him. Tadgh jumped out of the way.

"I'm convinced you're controlled by Kyle right now, madwoman," Tadgh growled.

"Stop your bickering, you two. I have a plan. If you want to help, then follow me to the library."

Ciaran turned around and walked quickly toward the library. Jo followed, stomping her feet. Tadgh glanced at Madeline, who was watching him closely. He put his head down and scurried toward the library. Madeline followed after taking a minute to glance around to be sure she sensed nothing from Kyle inside the house.

In the library, Ciaran opened a box. Inside the box were ten golden daggers.

"Holy cow, where did you get these?" Tadgh asked.

"I had them made for us," Ciaran said dryly. He picked up a dagger and handed it to Tadgh. "Feel it."

"Heavy," Tadgh said.

"They're made of our family gold, and it's top grade. Juliette mentioned that the Daimon Gate test is a transmutation process. It's equivalent to the most stringent process used in alchemy to produce pure gold."

"Pure gold against pure gold," Tadgh said more to himself than to anyone else. "Wow."

Ciaran gave a dagger to Madeline and Jo. "I hope they're not too heavy for you."

Madeline felt the dagger. "It's comfortable. Not heavy at all."

Ciaran spoke. "When I shot at Kyle, the bullets didn't seem to have much effect. The most damage Kyle sustained was in the swordfight with Richard. Ayana and Pete also fight with swords. I don't think Eudaiz's technology is too primitive to make guns. But I speculate that metal causes more damage to people from Eudaiz than gunpowder."

"So we take two each?" Tadgh asked. He grabbed two daggers and weighed them in his hands.

"Sorry I'm late," Zach said from the door. "Oh wow, haven't seen anything cooler than this in my entire life." Zach admired the daggers. "Are those for us?"

Ciaran nodded. "Two each." Ciaran handed two daggers to Zach.

"Wow, I could kill any creature with these," he said, obviously impressed.

"What can you tell us about the gate, Zach?" Ciaran asked.

"It's like a role play game, but it plays with your mind. My training was one-on-one. I was by myself with a lot of projections and reflections based on my own personal experiences. I don't know what will happen if a group goes through it. Will we each see different things?"

Ciaran shook his head. "I don't think so. I expect the scenarios will change for the whole group. But we'll have to face individual mental challenges, whatever they may be. I'll be leading and will need your support based on your roles. The ultimate goal will be to pass the gate as a group—or not pass at all."

"What about Kyle?" Zach asked.

"That's an unknown variable. We were told he's invincible. I don't think that's the case, but I haven't figured out how to kill him yet except to pass the gate and kill him on the other side. Ideally, if Jo and Tadgh could stall him on this side, we could pass the gate, get the power from the other side, and deal with Kyle later. But I'm not sure that's possible."

"It's not dangerous from this side to stall him," Jo said. "At least not for me."

"Excuse me. If you think I'm a burden, you're mistaken," Tadgh said.

"I didn't say that. But we're still not sure if Kyle can control you or not," Jo responded.

Before Tadgh said anything further, Ciaran cut in. "I agree with Jo, Tadgh. I don't think you should deal with Kyle at all. I regret letting you go this far. I wasn't thinking straight."

Tadgh lowered his voice. "You need me, Ciaran."

"I do. But I will not risk your life for this."

"He might not be able to affect me at all. Just like how it is with all of you."

"But we don't know that for sure, Tadgh," Madeline said.

"There's no way we can check this ahead of time, and before we are absolutely sure, I'm not willing to take the risk," Ciaran stated firmly. "I'm sending you home, Tadgh."

"The fuck I'll go."

Zach's phone buzzed. He ignored it. It buzzed again. He drew his phone out and glanced at the text message. "Fuck. It's Chloe. She tailed me here."

Zach charged out of the room.

CHAPTER 11

Tadgh looked at his hands and saw them shaking slightly. Was it excitement? Anxiety? He'd just figured out how to kill Kyle. It was definitely a risk. But hell, he had to do it. Kyle wasn't invisible at all. If he killed Kyle here, it would be a load off Ciaran and Madeline when they went through the Daimon Gate.

He followed everyone outside.

Chloe stood in the front garden. Her hair was tangled, her clothes were wrinkled, and she wore no makeup. Tears streamed down her face.

"There you are," Chloe said in a drunken voice. "You could have done better, Zach. We could have done better. You dumped me with a text? For her?" Chloe pointed toward Jo.

"No, no, Chloe. I . . . I don't know what to say."

"I know . . . You think I'm just a dumb blonde." She laughed through her tears.

"No, I don't think that at all, Chloe."

"But I love you, Zach," Chloe cried.

Jo approached. "You've got it all wrong, Chloe. I told you last night, I—"

Chloe whirled around, swinging her arms in the air. "You lied!" Chloe screamed at Jo.

Jo staggered back a step. Tadgh was right behind Jo. He snatched her and pulled her back. "Chloe, calm down," he said. "Zach is in enough trouble. If you love him, don't do this. It won't help him at all."

Chloe seemed to calm down a bit. Zach approached her and embraced her. She cried into his chest. Madeline had never before seen so much pain on his face.

"Can you tell me where you're going? Since when do we have secrets?" Chloe asked.

Zach bit his lip and said nothing.

Ciaran looked at Chloe's eyes. "Zach, be careful."

"He's here. Everyone, Kyle is here," Madeline alerted them.

Chloe's eyes went wild. She grabbed for the dagger Zach had tucked into his belt.

"Oh, Jesus, put it down Chloe," Zach said.

"Knock her out, Zach," Ciaran said.

"What?"

Chloe brandished the dagger and attacked Zach. He staggered backward. She screamed and charged forward at him. It would be easy for Zach to wrestle the dagger from Chloe and knock her out, but he couldn't do it. He grabbed her hand, but he couldn't strike her head.

Chloe roared again and gave Zach a kick which sent him rolling across the ground. She lurched forward, about to stab him.

Ciaran darted toward her. He could easily take her out.

Tadgh felt the sensation again. He knew what was coming. When Ciaran restrained Chloe, it would be his turn. Kyle would come to him.

Tadgh grabbed Chloe from behind. "Get away! Get away from Zach, or you'll regret this."

Tadgh heard a voice in his head now. "Let her do it. Let her kill him. He's your enemy."

Tadgh ignored the voice. He pulled Chloe away kicking and screaming. He could handle this. He ignored the voice. Tadgh could feel his nose bleeding. The voice was pounding in his head.

Tadgh grabbed Chloe's arm and bent it until the dagger was pointing at her neck.

"Tadgh, what are you doing?" Zach screamed.

"He's getting to Tadgh," Ciaran muttered. Madeline and Jo heard him.

"Oh, no!" Jo charged toward Tadgh and Chloe.

"Tadgh, I told Chloe last night that I love you. Tadgh, listen to me. Look at me," Jo said.

"I'm looking at you, goddamn it. He's not getting to me," Tadgh growled. His nose bled more. He continued to focus on blocking the pounding voice from his head.

"Cut her throat. Kill her. Kill the bitch," it said.

Chloe was crying now. Tadgh could feel her body shaking with fear. Jo stood in front of him. Tears rolled down her face. He wanted to wipe those tears away, but he knew better. As soon as he let go of Chloe, Jo might be the next person the beast asked him to kill.

Ciaran, Madeline, Jo, and Zach now approached Tadgh and Chloe.

Tadgh dragged Chloe, stepping backward.

"You hear me, Tadgh? Are you there?" Ciaran asked.

"Fuck yeah. I told you—it's not getting me."

"So why don't you let Chloe go?" Zach asked.

"Stay back, or I'll slit her throat, Zach."

"I don't know if you're still with us, Tadgh. The only way to prove that you understand what I'm saying and the implications of what you're doing is to let Chloe go," Ciaran said, stepping forward.

"Fuck it. Fuck you. Fuck all of this." Tadgh's head was pounding. His nose dripped blood.

"Slit her throat. She's a bitch. She asked Jo to leave you. Kill her," Kyle said.

"No, no, no!" Tadgh screamed out loud.

"It asked you to kill Chloe, didn't it, Tadgh?" Madeline asked. "I know you're still in there. I know you can control it. Otherwise, you would have killed her already."

"Let her go. I'll take care of it, Tadgh," Ciaran said.

"You mean you'll knock me out, Ciaran. How the fuck do you think I can face that humiliation?" Tadgh shook his head, hoping he could shake the beast's voice out.

"It's not a humiliation, Tadgh. It's a prize to let your pride go. You cannot take a life, Tadgh. You are the best fighter I've ever known. I'm proud of you. I can't lose you like this." Ciaran stepped forward again.

Tadgh dragged Chloe backward.

"Don't come any closer, Ciaran," he said.

"Kill her. Kill her. Kill her," Kyle chanted.

"I'll let her go. Step back, Ciaran." Suddenly, Tadgh's voice was calm and collected.

"Tadgh." Ciaran narrowed his eyes.

"I said step back. I'll let her go. But I won't let you knock me out."

"No," Ciaran said.

"You want her dead?" Tadgh asked.

"Kill her. Kill her. Kill her," the beast roared in Tadgh's head.

"Ciaran, step back. Please," Zach pleaded.

"Ciaran, Tadgh might hurt you. Move back," Madeline said.

"Yes, big brother. I might pierce this dagger through your beating heart. I don't want to do that. Step back. I promise I'll let Chloe go."

Ciaran took a step back.

"More," Tadgh directed.

Ciaran moved back one more step.

"Kill her. Let her go, and you will die. Kill her," Kyle roared again.

Tadgh released Chloe. She ran toward Zach.

As soon as Chloe left, a wave of sensation and sound took over Tadgh's mind for a brief moment. Then he blocked it out again.

"You fucking bastard. You will only get me in hell." Tadgh turned the dagger toward himself.

"No!" Ciaran yelled and charged at him. A wave of energy rushed past Ciaran, knocking him to the ground.

Tadgh felt a force of energy holding the dagger back an inch away from his body. Then on the blade of the dagger, blood appeared, dripping down.

It wasn't his blood. Someone was holding the dagger back.

The voice was loud in his head again. "Stay alive. Let go of the knife."

Tadgh smiled. A smile of victory. "Didn't see this coming, did you, Kyle?"

"Stay alive." Kyle pulled at the dagger.

"Oh, I haven't killed anyone on your command yet, have I? When your victim acts against your control, what will happen, Kyle? When your victims reverse your command, what will happen to your scores? If you want to know how to play the double-edged sword game, you should consult my brother. You're doomed."

Tadgh pressed the knife further. Blood streamed from Tadgh's body, soaking the handle of the dagger and revealing the hands of an old man.

Kyle roared. His image flickered. Flickered. Flickered. He revealed himself as an old man staring at the blood on his hands.

That was his real and true image in naked human eyes.

Kyle let go of the dagger. An electrical burning smell thickened the air.

"You are an ugly motherfucker," Tadgh said before he slumped to the ground. The world in front of him started to blur. But Tadgh's mind was as clear as it had ever been.

Kyle had lost his power of invisibility. Tadgh could see that Kyle was no longer invincible. He could not control Tadgh's mind now.

Tadgh saw an opportunity. But he had to be quick.

He looked up. Kyle was still dazed by the loss of his power. Tadgh pulled the dagger out of his body and charged at him. He stabbed Kyle with the dagger stained with his own blood.

Kyle roared in pain and slumped to the ground. He looked as if he was going to burst into flames. His body was almost transparent with burning fire which appeared to ignite from within him.

Jo darted toward Tadgh. She pulled him away from Kyle.

"Tadgh, please stay with me. I love you. Please."

Tadgh could feel her tears raining down on his face.

The others hurried toward them.

Behind Jo, Kyle rolled and stood up. He roared like a beast with all he had left. He swung his arm and created a powerful wedge of wind that swept Ciaran, Madeline, and Zach several feet away. Then he snatched Jo, swung her over his shoulder, and zoomed away as if into another dimension.

Tadgh faded away on the ground.

CHAPTER 12

They rushed Tadgh into the house. The hospital was too far away. They did all they could to stop the bleeding. Ciaran used whatever drugs he had on hand to treat his brother—drugs that Madeline did not know about and did not *want* to know about.

He ordered more medical equipment and drugs from his lab. He had what he'd requested airlifted to the mansion. His money and his well-built business empire came in handy at times, Madeline thought. As long as Tadgh survived, nothing else mattered.

Where had Kyle taken Jo?

Madeline looked out the window, gazing into the late afternoon. The sun was burning. Or maybe it was the anxiety in her that was burning. Kyle could not control Jo's mind, so what did he want? He seemed to have lost his invisibility. Maybe he'd lost his power. Madeline wasn't sure.

She needed Ciaran to make sense of what had just occurred—and to think of a solution. But she wouldn't be able to get Ciaran to think about anything else until Tadgh recovered.

Zach had taken Chloe back to the city. He had to find a way to secure her.

Tomorrow was the day of the gate opening. Madeline was sure it was going to be challenging. But she wasn't sure how they were going to survive *today*.

The sun had gone down now, and Tadgh had not yet opened his eyes. Ciaran could have airlifted Tadgh to the hospital, but for some reason, he did not. He hadn't talked to Madeline for hours while attending to Tadgh.

Ciaran worked on Tadgh and was on the phone with Doctor Thomas at the same time. It came down to a simple and final step now—Tadgh needed more blood. Ciaran and Tadgh shared a very rare blood type, but they did not store spare blood in the blood bank for convenient use overseas.

They also hadn't planned to bleed this much, Madeline thought.

Ciaran did not waste a moment thinking. He meticulously followed the steps and procedures as instructed by Doctor Thomas. There were times Madeline thought Ciaran would airlift Tadgh to a hospital or call in a medical professional. But she knew he trusted no one but Doctor Thomas and himself when it came to medical matters.

He drew his own blood and transfused it into Tadgh. It was a lot of blood. Madeline didn't need advanced medical knowledge to know that the amount of blood Ciaran extracted from himself was potentially dangerous.

Finally, the task was completed. Ciaran seemed to have done all he could. He sat down. Madeline approached the chair. She embraced him and kissed his tired face.

"I'd be very pleased if you'd take an hour to rest," Madeline said.

Ciaran kissed her. Madeline deepened the kiss. She knew he needed it. He needed her. Especially now. They held each other for a long moment, saying nothing.

A faint sound came from the bed.

Ciaran darted toward it. Tadgh opened his eyes. He was dazed and didn't seem to register what was going on around him. But he recognized Ciaran.

"You've lost a lot of blood, but you should be fine now," Ciaran said.

Tadgh closed his eyes again.

"No, no. Open your eyes, Tadgh."

There was no response.

"It's not working. I've missed something," Ciaran muttered and grabbed the phone. Madeline knew he wanted to call Doctor Thomas again. She doubted Doctor Thomas could do anything more at the moment.

Ciaran paused as if he'd just realized something. Then he spoke out loud, "Tadgh needed something more than blood. Something metaphysical."

Zach arrived and entered the room. "He's not awake yet?" he asked Madeline. She shook her head.

"Ayana!" Ciaran called out while pressing the crucifix on his arm.

"Don't waste your time. I've been doing that all night. She's not responding."

"Ayana!"

Nothing happened.

"If I can't fix my brother, I won't go anywhere near your pathetic gate," Ciaran growled to the air around him.

The air thickened and whirled. Sciphil Nine stepped out of the wind circle. It was not a holocast. He was a physical presence.

"Ciaran, the gate opening is in a few hours. Ayana cannot come. We know about the incident with Tadgh." Pete glanced at the bed.

"And what can you do about it?" Ciaran asked.

"What he did was very significant, Ciaran."

"It's most important that he stays alive. Do you have a suggestion?"

"Yes. I can give him some of my eudqi."

"Life force?" Ciaran nodded. "You're right. That's what he needs. What will it take for Tadgh to have your eudqi? What do you want me to do?"

"Nothing. It's an honor if I have Tadgh as my successor. When he becomes Sciphil Nine, he will have full access to the eudqi in his tower anyway. So this is a payment in advance."

"Then he'd say yes to it," Ciaran said.

"He has to accept the role himself. You know the drill, Ciaran."

"But he can't speak for himself right now, as you can see." Ciaran pointed toward the bed.

Madeline called out for Zach. "Could you send in a sound wave to wake him, Zach?"

Zach messed his hair up. "Oh, man. He's going to kick my ass for this." Zach concentrated. No response. He tried again. No response. He shifted. "Okay, hard head. How about this?" Zach mumbled and sent in a sound. Madeline had a feeling it would be an eardrum-shattering noise for Tadgh.

Tadgh screamed, convulsed, gasped, and opened his eyes.

Ciaran charged to the bed. "Tadgh, listen and say yes. Can you hear me?"

Tadgh was dazed. But he nodded.

Pete approached. "Tadgh LeBlanc, I now name you the successor of Sciphil Nine. Do you accept?"

"What the fuck?" Tadgh whispered.

"Just say yes, Tadgh." Ciaran shook him before he passed out again. "Say yes."

"What?" Tadgh was confused.

"Kyle is going to kill Jo. The only way you can save her is to accept this offer. You hear me?" Ciaran signalcd Pete.

Pete repeated, "Tadgh LeBlanc, I now name you the successor of Sciphil Nine. Do you accept?"

"Say yes, or Jo will die," Ciaran said.

"Yes, I accept," Tadgh said.

Pete reached out and burned a thumbprint into Tadgh's right forearm.

Tadgh passed out again.

CHAPTER 13

Jo opened her eyes and found herself in a small cell. It had been hours since she was snatched away from the mansion, away from her friends. The air had gotten colder as if the sun had gone down. There was no window in the cell. Her internal compass told her nothing regarding her whereabouts.

Jo looked at her dead cell phone, feeling hopeless. Kyle must have killed all of the phone network signals. Nobody would be able to track her now.

She ached everywhere and could not move her right arm.

Kyle had run for a long time at an incredibly supernatural speed. Jo had no idea how much ground he had covered—the world had been a blur when he ran. Jo remembered the strong wind and the electrical currents piercing her body.

If it were nighttime now, in a few hours, it would be another day—the day of the gate opening.

How was Tadgh? Was he alive? She needed him to be alive.

The heavy door slid open, and Kyle sauntered in with a tray of something that resembled edible food. His face reflected an extremely harsh life of over a hundred years, Jo thought.

He was tall and had the frame of a once-upon-a-time warrior. He was certainly very strong when he carried her, which was especially surprising after looking as if he had disintegrated on the ground.

"Do I look like I want food?" Jo asked.

"Young lady, you have to do what I say if you want your boyfriend to stay alive."

"What else can you do to him apart from the very obvious—use me as blackmail? He got you good, Kyle."

"By sacrificing himself? Do you really believe it was wise to do so? If you could go back in time, and you had a chance to stop him, would you still have let him do that?" Kyle smirked at Jo's silence.

He sat down next to her and tended to her injured arm. Jo shrugged him away. He grabbed her arm and held it still.

"This is infected. The wound was opened, and a very nasty chemical that your human body can't handle has gotten in there. I'll get someone with medical skills to tend to you. But our resources at this station are limited, so you won't see anything fancy."

"Which station?"

"You don't want to know, young lady. By the way, although my staff are not as pretty as you are, they're harmless. Don't be scared."

"I'm not on Earth? What the hell?"

Kyle shook his head. "You're better off not knowing. We're leaving soon. So eat your food and get your arm tended to."

"I'm not eating your food."

"Then be hungry."

Kyle turned to leave. Jo spoke to his back.

"Tadgh turned your lifetime work into shit, didn't he?"

Kyle stopped at the door and turned around slowly to face her. "You two are a perfectly matched couple. You are the only score I couldn't complete. I raped your soul, but you survived. You didn't kill yourself. You intrigue me, Jo. And that stubborn boyfriend of yours . . . when I tell him to kill, he lets people live. When I tell him to stay alive, he kills himself."

Kyle chuckled and shook his head. "The thing is, your individual actions will not help the greater cause. Ciaran is the key to that. His weakness is that he's human. And there's not much he can do about that."

He started to laugh. "He can't let go of human emotions, and that's what will destroy him. So I'm going to use you guys to dangle in front of Ciaran until the opportunity's ripe. Then I can destroy him with pleasure."

"Why?"

"It's hard to explain to a human. And I don't feel quite compassionate enough at the moment. But I have to admit that living among you guys for a long time, I've gained a bit of sentiment. So the short version of the answer is that Eudaiz belongs to me. Not to Bran, and thus not to Ciaran. And I *will* take back what's mine." He turned on his heel. "You can kill yourself to avoid being a burden to your friends. But again, let me get this through your thick skull. Your individual sacrifice can only harm the bigger picture." He walked out and slammed the door closed.

CHAPTER 14

"**N**ow what?" Ciaran asked Pete after Tadgh had accepted the successor position and passed out again.

"Where is the blood you're going to transfuse into him?" Pete asked.

"Already done."

"Well, do some more then."

"How much blood do you have to give, Ciaran?" Madeline asked although she knew it would make no difference.

"What blood type do you need?" Zach asked.

"The freak type, Zach. Don't worry. You won't have anything that matches," Madeline muttered.

Ciaran dragged the reading chair over to the bed and sat down.

"I have to do it directly. Not enough time to do it any other way." He connected all the necessary tubes into Tadgh's arm and his own. The blood started to draw, running from Ciaran to Tadgh. When the transfusion settled, Ciaran said. "How do you give your eudqi, Pete?"

Pete pointed to his right wrist.

"Madeline, there's a connector right there, on top of the pole. You have to use the needle—and be careful to keep the air out. Take blood from Pete, please."

He didn't ask if Madeline was able to do it. There was no one else he could rely on. Madeline nodded and performed the procedure.

The needle drew something from Pete's wrist. Something other than blood. It was a half-transparent silvery substance. It ran into the tube and mixed with Ciaran's blood. When there was enough, Pete pulled the needle out himself.

"That's enough to do the job. With his physique, he'll be as strong as superman. You have to distribute it throughout his system."

"You mean pumping it in using my blood?"

Pete nodded.

"How do I know when to stop?"

"He'll let you know." Pete smiled.

Madeline waited. Each minute felt like a decade. Ciaran sat back in the chair.

"What was significant about what Tadgh did?" Ciaran asked.

"We just found out new information about Kyle. What Tadgh did had to do with the metaphysics of Eudaiz and the Black Rock."

Ciaran raised an eyebrow. "Interesting," he said.

Zach mimed, "What the fuck?" at Madeline.

She shrugged. Within the short period of time she'd been with Ciaran, that was not the weirdest thing she had heard.

Pete continued. "To put it simply, while Eudaiz is built on a solid eudaimonic moral principal, the Black Rock is built on chaos. The core of their chaos theory is that if they can corrupt our moral ground, they can take over Eudaiz. Kyle betrayed Eudaiz for the Black Rock. His assignment was to prove that it was possible to corrupt innocence using his talent, which he achieved via Madeline. Tadgh disproved Kyle's result by killing himself under the influence of Kyle's control."

Ciaran laughed. "Backfire."

Pete nodded. "That means everything that Kyle achieved in the last three decades has been ruined. This has discredited him with the Black Rock, which is his only supply source. He has no other choice but to infiltrate the Daimon Gate tonight. If he makes it to Eudaiz, he'll devote his life to destroying it."

"Now that sucks," Zach moaned.

"We'll deal with him," Ciaran muttered, feeling quite queasy. His vision wavered. He shook his head and willed his eyes to open. Madeline saw the signs of exhaustion but said nothing.

"How much longer do you have to keep the blood flowing, Ciaran?" Madeline asked.

They heard a faint sound from the bed. Then Tadgh opened his eyes. He glanced around and grumbled, "What the hell is going on here?"

Ciaran pulled the needle from his arm. He went to the bed and pulled the tubes and needles from Tadgh.

"You were a bit sick. That's all. You're fine now. Can you get up?"

"Yeah . . ." Tadgh said.

It was incredible to see, given the condition he was in before, Tadgh sat up by himself. He winced with pain from where the stab wound was, but he got off the bed easily by himself.

Tadgh stood, looked around the room, looked at the thumbprint on his arm.

"Jo." He let out a gasp. "Where's Jo, Ciaran? You said she's going to die."

"I don't know where she is. Kyle's got her. I was preoccupied with you—"

"So nobody is looking for her? You told me I had to accept this Sciphil role to save her. Now you don't even know where she is? You bluffed me into accepting the Sciphil deal, didn't you, smart brother?"

Tadgh shoved Ciaran. Ciaran staggered back and fell onto the bedpost.

Tadgh was surprised that Ciaran fell so easily.

Madeline stepped toward Tadgh and gave him a slap across the face, sending him reeling into the wall behind him.

"Half of the blood in your body is Ciaran's. He located the substance that saved your life. All that because of your stupid heroic moment. I don't care how many universes you saved or destroyed. I don't care who you think you are, or what you're entitled to. At the moment, you are a dickhead."

"How long do we have until the gate opening?" Ciaran asked Pete.

"Four hours," Pete said.

"I'm going to need one of those for myself," Ciaran said dryly and walked out of the room. Madeline scurried after him.

Zach shrugged. "I'm worried about Jo, too. But I agree with Madeline about you. If I rephrased what she said, it wouldn't be as gentle. If I repeated what she did, no amount of superhero juice would keep you standing." Zach walked away, leaving Tadgh and Pete alone in the room.

CHAPTER 15

The cell door slid open. Jo crawled into a corner to guard herself against the two creatures strolling in.

They walked on two legs, so Jo assumed they were at least at the ape level in the food chain. But their bodies were hideous, Dr. Frankenstein-looking creations. Although Frankenstein's work wasn't pretty, Jo thought, it was no comparison to what she saw now.

One creature had a combination of multicolored skins. The other was made of the face and body parts of many different animals. The body parts looked as if they were the leftovers from a cannibal's meal.

They said nothing. They grabbed Jo, ignoring her physical protests and verbal insults. One held her down, and the other treated her arm. They finished quickly. As much as Jo hated to admit it, she felt an instant relief from the pain.

A moment later, Kyle entered. "We have to leave now. I normally travel on foot, but I don't want to hurt you again, so we'll take the capsule this time."

"The capsule?"

Kyle did not answer. He snatched Jo, pulling her out of the cell, and shoved her into a round, metal cabin that indeed looked like a capsule. There was no window, so Jo could not orient herself. In what seemed like only a few seconds, the capsule opened. Kyle pulled her out of the capsule, and they walked into a dirt tunnel that went underground.

Upon their exit, they climbed up the stairs of a basement where hay was clustered and tools were piled up against wooden panels. When they came out of the basement, she saw a familiar sight—a farmhouse and a barn. And farm animals. Jo was sure they were Earth animals. They looked friendly, which was a bonus. She had never had a good relationship with cows and sheep. But at the moment, she loved them. She smiled graciously at a cow nearby.

A car was parked in the distance. The driver got out and opened the door at the back for Kyle and Jo. Further away, Jo spotted a line of ten cars and saw armed men standing around. If they were Kyle's men, then her friends would be outnumbered at the gate.

These men were worse than the soldiers at Fountains Abbey. The soldiers had been human—these men were not. They were like zombies, but maybe slightly better-looking. Jo no longer had her phone. She didn't know how to alert Madeline and the others about this little army.

She stumbled on her heels and fell next to one of the zombie-ish men. As he crouched to help her up, she snatched his phone. When they got to the car, Kyle opened the door for her. He reached his hand out and said, "Give it to me."

"Give what?" She played dumb.

"You don't want to upset me now, Jo. Give it back."

Jo grumbled some profanity and shoved the phone into Kyle's hand. She got into the car and sank into the passenger seat. Kyle stepped in after her and sat next to her with a crooked smile on his face. Jo shifted and moved away.

"I'm not *that* scary," Kyle said.

"Nope. Not at all. You're a saint. I bet my life on it," she said and looked out the window.

She tried her best to keep a neutral expression and show a small sign of vulnerability. On the inside, she was doing a victory dance. In addition to the phone, she had also stolen a pocket knife from the zombie gangster and was overjoyed to feel its weight in her pants' secret pocket.

CHAPTER 16

On the other side of town, Zach held the wheel. Tadgh was in the front with him, and Madeline and Ciaran sat in the back. They were heading toward an old gold mine outside Ballarat, a small historic Victorian town.

Ciaran obviously needed more than an hour to recoup, Tadgh contemplated. Otherwise, he would never have let Zach take the wheel.

Tadgh couldn't drive because if he did, they would never get to the site in time. He worried about Jo. But he had a feeling that she would be fine. She was smart and resourceful. She knew how to handle herself—even if he had to go through the

Daimon Gate with Ciaran as the successor of Sciphil Nine and leave her alone on Earth.

Tadgh shook his head. He worried about Ciaran more.

His brother sat in the back, saying nothing. That was a sign that Ciaran was utilizing every waking moment to regain his strength. Tadgh regretted that his action had caused so much trouble. He wondered how much longer it would be until he had even a fraction of the maturity his brother had.

Madeline pulled Ciaran so that he leaned on her and lay his head on her shoulder. She liked the feel of their bodies together. Leaning on her shoulder, Ciaran nuzzled into the nape of Madeline's neck. He kissed her neck and gave it a little bite. Madeline chuckled. She turned his face toward her and kissed him.

An hour later, they were at the site. It was forty minutes before sunset.

"Do you see the gate?" Ciaran asked.

"Well, that's the gate of an old gold mine. I assume the Daimon Gate will be a bit grander," Zach said.

There was nothing around them except the bare hills. The cattle were quietly heading home, single file. Everything seemed to be settling in preparation for the sunset.

They got out of the car.

Tadgh looked at Ciaran as if he wanted to say something. Madeline saw the hint and went to talk to Zach.

Ciaran stood leaning against the trunk of the car. Tadgh approached. "I'm sorry about what I said and did at the mansion, Ciaran. I don't know what got into me."

"Don't worry about it. I know what it feels like to be left out."

"What?"

"You knew you were susceptible to Kyle's mind tricks. Nobody wants to be the weak link, Tadgh. I understand that. And the fact that I threatened to send you home didn't help. I'm sorry for that. But I wish you'd told me."

Tadgh nodded. "Should've, could've, didn't."

"I suppose I'm not exactly easy to talk to."

"You've got that right." Tadgh chuckled.

"Let's leave that behind us, shall we?" Ciaran gave Tadgh a pat on the shoulder. "You're my little brother. It's my job to look out for you."

The air cooled down quickly.

The opening time was approaching. The sun began sinking behind the hills.

They got back into the car. Ciaran took the wheel this time. They lowered the car windows to feel the movement of the air.

It was coming.

The air thickened. They heard a rumbling sound. But there was no sign of a storm.

The rumbling sound came from behind them.

"Kyle's here," Madeline said. She could sense him.

Ciaran looked in the rearview mirror and saw a line of cars coming toward them.

"I suppose they're real cars with real people," he muttered to himself. Ciaran put the car into gear quickly and turned around in the blink of an eye.

"Ten against one, coward," Ciaran said. "Got your guns ready, people?" Ciaran asked. Before getting a response, he turned the steering wheel and drove in a circle. He fishtailed and smashed into one of the cars at the far end. Before the car driver could register the impact, Zach took him out with a bullet.

Ciaran continued to drive in a circle. The nine cars left made a bigger circle so that Ciaran could not break away. Bullets rained on them, but most missed the car because of the speed at which Ciaran was driving.

"Get two more will you?" He charged at one car and swirled his steering wheel in the last second to sneak in between the two running cars. Before they could react, Tadgh and Zach took down the two cars.

Cars drove around and around at incredible speeds. Dirt and grass flew everywhere. Ciaran was too fast for the other cars to see or anticipate his location. They couldn't even see which way his car was facing, let alone shoot at it.

Ciaran drove head-on into a car. He said to Madeline, who was sitting in the front with him, "Can you take him down before we hit?" It was a rhetorical question. Regardless of whether she could do it or not, he maintained his head-on path and assumed she could shoot the other car.

Madeline pointed the gun and shot, taking the driver out.

"Two sides, Tadgh and Zach."

Ciaran maneuvered in an S around and behind the six remaining cars. As soon as he got close enough, Tadgh and Zach fired.

In the grass and dirt, and amid the chaotic sounds of car engines, they took the remaining cars out quickly.

Ciaran stopped the car. Madeline got out without realizing that a man behind them had stood up and grabbed a gun.

In the blink of an eye, Zach sent a sound signal into the man's head. He grunted out a sound, grabbed his ears, and had his head blown off by a bullet from Tadgh's gun.

The air thickened and started whirling.

"The gate is opening," Zach said.

They checked their daggers and headed toward the gate of the old gold mine. The air in front of it stirred more strongly. The wind circle sucked in objects from the immediate area and ejected them in all directions.

In the strong wind, blue and white light beams swirled around like gigantic cylinders. It was similar to the tornado Juliette had created, but this one was colorful and much bigger.

"What now, Zach? Should we just walk right in there?" Ciaran asked.

"Wait. Ayana has to take us in."

In the middle of the wind circle, Ayana appeared, a gracious smile on her face. She stepped outside the circle. "Welcome to you all. Follow me."

Before they could take a step, Ayana swung her sword and pointed at a dark corner. "Come out," she said.

A whirl of black dirt and wind came. It created a blade of wind and knocked everyone on the ground except Ayana.

Kyle appeared. "Thanks for opening the gate. Long time no see, Ayana. You are still as beautiful as ever."

Kyle swung his arm at Ayana. Ayana pushed up her sword to block. The wind circle shrank instantly and started to collapse on her. Ayana stabbed her sword into the ground and regained her stance. The circle opened again.

"You are quite busy, I see." Kyle smirked. "Let me give you a hand to get rid of some uninvited passengers for the gate."

He charged toward Ciaran with an enormous black sword. Ciaran pulled out his daggers and blocked the sword. Tadgh kicked at Kyle and pulled his daggers out as well. Zach charged at him with two daggers pointing straight toward his heart.

Kyle swung his sword, throwing Ciaran several feet away. Tadgh's legs were still numb from his kicks, which apparently did no damage at all to Kyle.

Kyle swung his sword at Zach in response to his attack. Zach's daggers were blown away, and he fell on the ground rolling.

Kyle stepped toward Zach. "I only want the LeBlanc brothers dead. You are a guest of the gate, so I'll spare your life."

"Fuck you," Zach said.

"You're welcome."

Then Kyle roared in pain. Madeline had stabbed her two daggers into his heart from the back. He swung around and threw Madeline away.

"Kids, run inside. I'll close the gate," Ayana called out.

Madeline, Ciaran, Zach, and Tadgh stood up and raced toward the gate.

Kyle roared again. He pulled the two daggers out and threw them at Madeline.

They made impact. Madeline fell. Blood pooled quickly on the ground around her.

"No, no, Ayana, I can't let her die," Ciaran yelled. He held Madeline in his arms.

"Take her inside. This is the transitional zone. Take her inside the gate. The dimension will change, and she won't die," Ayana said.

Ciaran carried Madeline, charging against the wind toward the gate.

Kyle reeled away.

Zach and Tadgh ran toward the gate.

From the darkness, Kyle came back, holding Jo in front of him as a human shield.

"The girl will die if you take her inside the gate. She can't protect you, Kyle," Ayana said.

Zach and Tadgh turned around.

"No, you two must come inside. I can't hold this open any longer," Ayana commanded.

"I have to get Jo," Tadgh said.

Kyle pushed against the wind toward the gate.

"The girl will die. Uninvited guests will die by the light of a thousand lightning bolts. Don't do that, Kyle," Ayana said.

"Let me in, or I'll kill her right now."

"You're beyond redemption."

Kyle merely put on an evil smile.

Jo looked at Tadgh. She saw him trying to run toward her, but he was being held back by Zach. She saw Madeline being carried by Ciaran, who was racing madly toward the gate. Zach dragged Tadgh, trying to make it to the gate. Jo wanted to smile at them, but she could not. She wanted to tell them not to worry, but her body would not obey her. A sensation ran down her spine.

Then Zach pulled Tadgh inside.

Kyle pushed in.

Ayana withdrew her sword and disappeared.

The door shut.

Darkness.

CHAPTER 17

Ciaran drew in the fresh air and opened his eyes. His face was pressed against the wet, cold grass, and his hands gripped a bunch of wildflowers. Fear flooded back into his mind. *Madeline!* He scrambled to his feet.

A few feet away, Madeline lay on the ground, staring into the big eyes of a young deer. The light brown deer with white dots on his back was licking her face. Ciaran felt delirious. He shook his head.

The gate opening had happened so fast. He couldn't recall the events. But he didn't want to recall anyway as that would include the scene of the two daggers stabbing into Madeline.

He couldn't take that pain. Not again. He now understood what it had felt like for her at Fountains Abbey when he was shot. It was the most helpless feeling he had ever experienced.

Madeline sat up. The deer ran away. The two daggers now lay beside her. Neither her blood nor Kyle's was on them.

Surrounding them was a tall grass meadow wedged right against the edge of a forest. Madeline looked around. Before she could register the new world they had entered, Ciaran planted a kiss on her lips.

A few feet away, Zach and Tadgh sat up. "We're inside the gate," Ciaran said.

"Now we just have to get out the other end, don't we? Piece of cake," Zach said sarcastically.

Tadgh glanced around. Ciaran knew he was looking for a sign of Jo. "Do you know where to find Jo, Ciaran?" Tadgh asked.

"Kyle and Jo would be here, too. In this dimension. The Daimon Gate is a dimension, a world in and of itself," Ciaran responded.

"Ayana said she could be . . ." Zach stumbled on the words.

"No, Zach. She's not a guest of the gate. But Kyle wanted to use her as a human shield. He'd have a way to keep her alive. I don't know how, but I'm sure she is not dead as a result of entering the gate," Ciaran reassured.

"But . . ." Tadgh protested.

"Tadgh, I know you're worried. Everyone here is. But we have to survive to find her. If you have a better solution, I'd be happy to listen," Ciaran stated firmly. He had to stay firm to calm Tadgh's nerves. He needed to take the whole group through this alive, and there was no room for error.

Tadgh said nothing.

"So what are we dealing with here, Zach, based on your training?" Ciaran asked.

"Well, it's not a hologame. So we could die for real or get lost in oblivion forever."

"So the challenges will come to us?" Ciaran said.

"Exactly."

"What about the duration?" Tadgh asked.

"I think we have dimensional time in here. Which means we could spend a long time in challenge, but to the world outside from both ends of the gate, it would be just a short moment," Ciaran said.

"In my training, Ayana showed me a range of scenarios of obstacles and dangers based on my past experiences. For example, I have aquaphobia. There was a scenario where I had to fight a bunch of stupid fish underwater. The idea is to conquer your fear."

"You don't swim?" Tadgh snorted.

"I do—and quite well if you must know. But it doesn't make me like diving. You don't have a phobia?"

"He has tachophobia, a fear of speed," Ciaran said.

"Thank you for advertising it, Ciaran!" Tadgh protested.

Ciaran shrugged. "The more we know, the better we can plan, Tadgh. And you, Madeline?"

"I don't have a phobia. Not that I know of. And you?"

"Same." Ciaran smiled and winked at her.

"Is it going to be a combined scenario? Everyone's fears combined into one challenge? Should we list our fears and plan how to deal with them?" Madeline asked.

Ciaran smiled. "I wish it was that simple. Juliette said this is similar to an alchemical transmutation process. In principle, if we pass the gate, we will be purified and become better people. It's like making gold."

"Dandy, cleanse me!" Zach mumbled.

"Making gold is possible. Making me a better person is a fantasy," Tadgh stated.

Ciaran contemplated and said, "We have to take one thing at a time. In principle, if it's an alchemical transmutation, we are looking at three general stages—Black, White, and Red. I assume you don't want the ancient terminologies such as Nigredo, Albido, or Rubedo..."

"No, no, thank you. English, please! I can deal with some French maybe but nothing weirder than that," Tadgh said.

"In the Black stage, there will be a lot of heat. It's called the calcination process. You can work it out from the word."

"Burn us to ashes," Madeline mumbled.

There was a rumble underground, and the ground shook.

"Shit. What's that?" Zach said.

"Welcome to Nigredo," Ciaran muttered and grabbed Madeline's hand.

The sound came from the right at the far end of the meadow. Ciaran pointed toward the bush on the left.

"This will fall. Run!"

CHAPTER 18

They charged toward the forest. The meadow collapsed and peeled off, layer by layer, right behind them.

In the jungle, they could smell wood burning.

"This is definitely the calcination stage," Ciaran said while running. Then he stopped. Everyone else stopped, too.

"We can't run aimlessly." Ciaran concentrated. He spoke quickly, "There will be fire everywhere. We are looking for the sign of a salamander. If we see it, that means we have passed the black stage."

"There." Madeline pointed toward the right where they saw the shadow of a reptile tail.

They ran toward the retreating shadow. Trees on both sides and behind them burst into flames. The fire did not blow in the wind. Instead, it was restrained within the trees, making them gigantic burning coals.

They turned the corner where the shadow of the tail had reflected before them and faced burning walls of fire.

It was a maze of flames.

"Oh, no, not again," Zach mumbled.

"What?" Tadgh said.

"I was put into a maze before. It wasn't a burning one. But it was tricky."

"How did you get out?" Ciaran asked.

"I couldn't. My friend worked it out. But there will be moving walls and moving paths," Zach said.

"Tadgh, your job. We're looking for signs of water. Not earth or air. Water. If we keep seeing fire, we're heading in the wrong direction." Ciaran pointed toward the burning maze.

"Me? What if I get it wrong?" Tadgh exclaimed.

"You won't. You're good at this. Work it out."

Ciaran speculated the answer was on the right. He was not as good at matrices as Tadgh, but he knew enough.

Tadgh thought and then pointed toward the left. "Three blocks, left, left then right."

Ciaran had a strong feeling that Tadgh was wrong. But he had given his brother the task. He had to follow through with it. "I'll check it out," Ciaran said.

"No, Ciaran, I'll do it," Tadgh said.

"I lead the group. I'll check. You stay." Ciaran grabbed Madeline and kissed her quickly. "I love you," he whispered and darted to the left.

Madeline knew it was a goodbye kiss. She saw it in his eyes. She knew he thought it was the wrong direction. But he followed because Tadgh had said so. He did it to show his faith and confidence in his brother. Madeline felt a lump in her throat and prayed that her instinct was wrong this time.

As soon as Ciaran turned the corner, the firewall moved and closed the path.

"Fuck!" Tadgh said. "Wrong path."

Ciaran saw the wall close behind him. He kept running in the direction he feared was the wrong way. Deep down, he knew he'd pull this off.

Left. Left. And right. And a dead end.

The last wall closed behind him, enclosing Ciaran in a burning corner with his ophidiophobia, fear of snakes. It was a phobia so ordinary that Ciaran had never cared to admit to it.

He had never let the fear defeat him. He had attacked it with a ferocity, and no one would ever have known that he had a phobia at all.

From a corner, a snake rose slowly. Despite the heat from the walls, Ciaran felt a chill run down his spine.

"Not now," Ciaran mumbled to himself. He would not freak out. He would do what he had done before—he would kill the snake.

Ciaran pulled out his daggers. He could do this with ease. Two swings in opposite directions, and the snake would be sliced into pieces.

But Ciaran recognized that this was no ordinary snake. It was a legendary gatekeeper, a serpent with a red snake body and a wide-jawed dragon's head.

It rose as high as Ciaran's head. It slithered around, back and forth, watching him. It went around him and stopped in front of him.

One swing, and he could kill it. That was how he normally handled his fear, but this situation was a lot more difficult, Ciaran thought.

Gatekeeper, Ciaran contemplated. He would need the ticket or the key. Ciaran used the dagger on his right hand to pull up the sleeve on his left arm, revealing the golden crucifix tattoo. From this angle, it looked more like a key.

Ciaran thought the snake looked happy—if it was possible to deduce such emotion from a snake. It slid around in front of his left arm as if admiring the crucifix.

Then the snake opened its mouth wide and bit down on Ciaran's arm.

A searing pain shocked Ciaran's brain and made him almost pass out. He dropped the dagger in his left hand.

The snake pulled away. On his arm was not an ordinary snakebite mark with two fang holes. Instead, there was a round circle of holes around the crucifix. It looked as though the key was inserted into a lock.

Ciaran staggered back. His left arm immediately felt numb.

It was the venom. But Ciaran knew what to do. He swung the right hand dagger. He had to give up his left arm, or he would die.

CHAPTER 19

Madeline snarled, "Tadgh, which way is the right direction? Ciaran got the wrong one, and that path's closed." Fear clawed at her. Beads of sweat streamed down her face.

Tadgh whirled around and around, looking at the moving paths and walls.

"Stop spinning. You're making me dizzy, Tadgh," Zach said.

Madeline closed her eyes and tried to connect to Ciaran's mind. She tried to trace his thoughts the way she had on Earth.

Nothing.

Her psychic ability didn't work here.

Don't panic, she said to herself. *Just use your ordinary human sense of direction.* She blocked all of the moving parts in front of her out of her mind and concentrated, tracing Ciaran's physical steps.

***

Ciaran wanted to cut off his left arm. He had to stop the venom from spreading into his heart. But the snake swung up its tail quickly and grabbed Ciaran's right arm with it. It squeezed hard so that Ciaran dropped the dagger to the ground.

The snake spoke to him.

"Keep the venom. You'll need it."

Then the snake vanished. Ciaran slumped to the ground while the searing pain stabbed at his head. The wall slid open. Madeline, Tadgh, and Zach stormed in. Madeline grabbed Ciaran.

"Where does it hurt? Are you burned? Where?"

Ciaran pulled his sleeve down to cover the snake bite and stood up. "I'm fine. This is the wrong way."

"Yes, I'm sorry," Tadgh said.

"So where to now?" Ciaran said.

"You're asking me again?"

"Who else should I ask? Madeline? Zach?"

Madeline and Zach shook their heads.

Tadgh literately recoiled from Ciaran's gaze. Ciaran waited. Then Tadgh pointed. "All right. That way. I don't want to die in here."

They ran in the opposite direction this time.

The burning walls opened up.

"This looks more like it," Madeline said.

Ciaran shook his left arm to check that it was still attached to his body.

In front of them was a river of dark water flowing into an underground cave. A line of disks sailed over the water like a conveyor belt. All of the discs turned at the corner.

"It looks like the only way out," Tadgh said, pointing at the discs flying by at an incredibly fast speed.

"We don't want to get into that water," Zach said, staring down at his worst nightmare.

"The fire is closing in behind us. We have to jump now," Madeline said.

Ciaran assessed his trajectory and jumped onto a disk.

"It's fine."

And then the disc swung around the corner.

Madeline jumped onto the next one.

Zach took a step back to get momentum and then jumped.

Tadgh looked at the discs. They were too fast for him. "Come on!" Zach's voice echoed back. Tadgh wanted to close his eyes but couldn't because he would miss the disc when he jumped. He clenched his teeth and jumped onto the next one.

Each disc could hold only one person. It was moving too fast for Tadgh. He was on all fours and gripping the edge of the disc.

In front of Tadgh, Zach's disc became unstable and flipped around.

Zach fell.

Tadgh grabbed him before he hit the water. The two of them hung on tightly to Tadgh's disc.

The disc turned the corner, and they immediately hit a waterfall. It was so sudden that both Tadgh and Zach were flushed off the disc.

Tadgh's body hit a hanging rock. He fell, unconscious, dropping down into the dark water of the river below. Zach was left hanging onto a rock. He saw Tadgh fall.

"Oh, come on!" Zach moaned. Zach let go of his rock and dove into the dark water.

It was dark and quiet below the surface of the water. His fear was not important right now. A life was on the line. He dove deeper. And there, he found Tadgh, sinking like a stone.

CHAPTER 20

Ciaran grabbed the rocky edge of a wall. Madeline was swimming toward him. He reached his hand out and grabbed her. He swung her up on the rock and looked back to the far dark corner.

There was no sign of Tadgh and Zach.

***

Zach grabbed Tadgh and pushed him up to the surface. Tadgh was breathing. Zach supported his head, keeping it above the water, and swam along with the current. They were in a dark cave.

Mysterious hanging rocks were illuminated by a spooky dim light, and it looked like a thousand beady eyes were staring at him. They acted like torches. Otherwise, Zach wouldn't be able to see anything.

In the distance, Zach saw a small strip of rocks. Ciaran and Madeline were standing on top. He swam toward them.

Ciaran and Madeline helped pulled Tadgh up onto the rock.

"He hit a rock when we fell. He's all right," Zach said.

Tadgh coughed up some water, then he opened his eyes and rolled over to sit up. He rubbed his head.

"Are you okay now?" Ciaran asked.

Tadgh nodded. "Hey, thanks for grabbing me," he said to Zach.

"Not a problem. Same goes. I hitched a ride on your disc. If you were by yourself, you wouldn't have fallen," Zach said.

"Ciaran found a way out," Madeline said.

"Oh yeah!" Zach narrowed his eyes. "Not under the water again?"

Ciaran smiled and nodded. He pointed ahead. "Around that corner is the mouth of the cave, where the river flows out to an opening. However, the mouth of the cave is closed by a gate."

"You mean a manmade gate?" Tadgh asked. "If it's manmade, exactly what is being locked in here?"

"It's not going to be anything friendly, so I'd try not to think about it if I were you," Madeline said.

"The handle to lift the gate is underwater. By my gauge, it might take all four of us to turn it," Ciaran said. His voice shook a bit, and his teeth started to chatter with the cold.

"Okay, let's go and get it done then," Zach said.

Ciaran leaned on the rock wall, gesturing that he needed a moment. He sat down.

Madeline put her arm around him. "What's wrong, Ciaran?"

"Nothing."

His lips turned purple. Ciaran knew the snake poison had spread throughout his body. He was surprised it hadn't killed him already.

Madeline looked at Ciaran's face. "Tell me, Ciaran."

Ciaran pulled up his sleeve to show the snake bite. The wound had turned black now as well as the area around it. "The snake left me a souvenir," Ciaran said.

"Oh, Jesus Christ!" Madeline cried out.

Tadgh grabbed his dagger.

Ciaran gestured Tadgh to stop. "I could have done it myself. But the snake said I'd need it."

"It meant you needed the poison?" Tadgh said.

Ciaran found it hard to talk now. He was too cold. "We have to get out of here," he said. He got into the water and started swimming toward the gate's handle.

The metal bars of the gate stared at them in challenge. There was only a foot between the water's surface and the ceiling of the cave. The water was not too deep. It was more of a tunnel than a cave.

The wheel to open the gate had four handles. They all dove under the water, grabbed a handle, and turned.

The door shifted up an inch. They came up for air and dove down for another round. Each time, they managed to shift the gate up only an inch.

Suddenly, they felt a strange movement in the currents. In the dim light, they could see a pair of beady eyes deep inside the tunnel.

They surfaced. There was nowhere for them to go. They couldn't go back inside to the rocks.

"What is it, Ciaran?" Madeline asked.

"I think it's some kind of sea monster," Ciaran responded.

"Like a seahorse?" Tadgh asked.

"But this isn't the ocean," Zach said.

"I don't think it's here by choice. It's locked in here with us," Ciaran said.

"What are we supposed to do now?" Madeline asked.

They felt the water being sucked into the cave, rushing from the river outside, gushing through the bars and flowing toward the monster. They grabbed the bars of the gate. The suction was incredibly strong. The water brought with it whatever was in the river.

"It's feeding time. Great," Ciaran muttered.

CHAPTER 21

Ciaran ducked his head under the water to take a look at the animal. Then he came up again.

"It's going to feed now. It will open its mouth and create a strong current to suck everything in. We have to open the gate and get out as quickly as we can. But I don't think we can handle the gate and the current at the same time. So Madeline, Tadgh, and I will open the gate, and Zach, you have to distract it with your sound wave."

"How?"

"I don't know—that's *your* job," Ciaran said and dove down to the handle. Tadgh and Madeline did the same.

Zach dove under the water along with them. He looked at the sea monster. He had never seen a fish that ugly in all his life—the mouth of a whale, alligator eyes, and a scaled body.

It stared at Zach. He stared back. Then, looking bored, the sea monster turned and opened its mouth as wide as the tunnel.

The current started to flow in.

Zach concentrated and shot out a sound wave that he thought the monster would hate. Nothing happened. The current grew stronger.

The gate lifted one more inch.

Ciaran, Madeline, and Tadgh were not coming up for more air. They kept turning the handle.

One more inch.

Zach shot again. It hit something. The monster startled and shook. It looked angry.

Shit. If I make it angry, it might eat more. Suck everyone into that ugly mouth, Zach thought. He sent out another sound.

The gate lifted one more inch.

The monster grew angrier. They heard a high-pitched sound, followed by a low rumbling sound, and then felt a gigantic rush of current.

They couldn't keep turning the gate now. They hung onto the bars as tightly as they could. The current drew in fish, rocks, logs, and many other things from the river.

Zach couldn't send any more sounds. He hung onto the gate, too. They didn't know how long they could hold on.

Ciaran had only one functional arm now. The other had been numb with the pain and the snake poison.

The current grew stronger by the second. Ciaran knew the first person it swept away would be Madeline. She couldn't possibly have as strong a grip as the men. He had to do something about it.

Ciaran let go of the gate. The current drew him toward the monster's mouth.

Ciaran pulled out his dagger and cut his left arm. The black poison released quickly into the water and flowed into the monster's mouth. Before Ciaran's body hit the mouth of the monster, it clamped its jaws shut.

The current stopped.

The monster did not move. It looked as if it had passed out.

Ciaran surfaced and drew in a breath. "Bon appétit!" he said and quickly swam back to the handle. The four of them dove again and turned the handle.

One more inch. And one more. Finally, they created a gap just large enough for their bodies to slide under.

Suddenly, the monster rumbled. It roared and charged at the gate.

Tadgh was the last person to slide through the gap. As soon as he slid through, the monster's teeth snapped at the steel bars.

They kicked to the surface of the river just before dusk.

Ciaran was as white as a sheet. He didn't know how long he would last. Madeline grabbed him and kicked toward the bank of the river. It was growing cold quickly. A few feet from the bank, they saw movement in a bush.

A red human-sized lizard stood up on two legs and ambled toward them.

Tadgh, Zach, and Madeline drew their weapons.

"No, it's a salamander," Ciaran said. "We've passed the black stage."

He walked toward the lizard. He tried his best not to reel although his knees wanted to buckle. "Is that correct?" Ciaran did not know why he expected the lizard talk to him. It just stared. There was something in its eyes that he recognized. He didn't know what it was. But those weren't a reptile's eyes.

Ciaran pulled his sleeve up. His left arm had now turned black. He revealed the crucifix and the bite mark.

"Is this what you're after?"

The salamander looked at the wound. It stuck out its reptile tongue and licked at the wound. Then it stood up and looked Ciaran in the eyes.

"Have we passed the black stage?" Ciaran asked.

The salamander nodded.

Ciaran slumped and passed out cold on the ground.

Madeline darted toward him. The salamander hissed at her. It whirled back and forth and sucked at the cut on Ciaran's arm. Soon, his arm returned to its normal color.

The salamander sauntered away and disappeared into the bush.

Madeline hugged Ciaran, who was shivering as the temperature continued to drop.

"Can you two make a fire?" Madeline said.

"Like a campfire?" Zach asked, looking hopeless. "We don't have a lighter."

"I can do it," Tadgh said and started gathering dry branches.

"Didn't Ciaran say this was the just the first stage?" Zach asked.

Madeline nodded at the rhetorical question and smiled.

Tadgh shook his head and concentrated on making the fire.

CHAPTER 22

The dawn came suddenly, casting light onto a reflective surface of ice. Ciaran opened his eyes to find himself lying next to Madeline, her arms still wrapped around him. They were no longer on the river bank. Instead, in front of them was a magnificent and endless snowfield.

Everything was white, including the sky.

Ciaran reached over and kissed Madeline. She woke and responded to his warm kiss.

Tadgh and Zach awoke nearby.

"Holy cow," Tadgh gasped when he saw the snowfield.

"Just like in a hologame, isn't it, Ciaran?" Zach asked.

"Except it's not a game," Ciaran said in response. He looked out at the snowfield and up to the white sky. Ciaran continued, "This is the White stage, everyone. While the Black stage focused on physical aspects, this stage is more of a mental test."

"Will it be more difficult than the last one?" Tadgh asked.

"It reflects personal experiences. I'd say it's more difficult for some and easier for others. Just in case we get separated, you need to know that this stage uses air and earth elements, and it's prone to catastrophic effects. It doesn't mean we're dealing with an apocalypse. It means, mentally, it will test our capability to make significant decisions. Those that change your life and the lives of others."

Ciaran looked at everyone. The lack of responses worried him.

"Am I understood?"

"Yep, sure," Zach said.

"Yes, Ciaran. Why do you seem more worried about this stage than the last?" Madeline asked.

"In alchemy, there are two small steps in this stage—separation and conjunction. In the Black stage, everything is burned so that only the essence remains. In the White stage, we have to focus on separating the good parts and the bad parts, and then joining the good parts together. For me, it's more difficult because there is no clear boundary between good and bad."

"Just stick together. We'll combine our brain power, I guess," Tadgh said, although he had absolutely no idea how he would go about choosing between good and bad. This was more Ciaran's kind of game than his.

"What's the sign for us passing this stage, Ciaran?" Zach asked.

"We may see a rainbow or a peacock's tail," Ciaran said.

Tadgh shook his head.

They headed deeper into the snowfield. They didn't have to walk for long before they found an ice castle located imposingly in the middle of the snowfield. The wide entrance to the castle was open and inviting. It was quiet. There was no sign of anyone—no guards, no soldiers, no people.

"Is that sleeping beauty's castle?" Zach asked jokingly.

"I think we're about to see Snow White," Tadgh said.

"I don't have a fairytale feeling at all. I think it's a white pyramid, and we're about to be chased by snow mummies," Madeline said.

"I'm afraid Madeline is right. Not sure about the mummies. But this is a test—or a trap, to be precise. Still, we have to go in," Ciaran said.

"That sucks. Knowing it's a trap and still having to go in," said Zach.

They crossed a small, snow-covered bridge to enter the castle. It was like any other picturesque castle that Madeline had seen in England. Except that everything here was icy.

They walked into the main hall. The magnificent round hall was decorated by ice pillars and white roses. A couple of white swans swam in a small pond in the middle of the hall.

Two doormen in white uniforms pushed open a gate opposite them to reveal a long corridor inside. The doormen smiled at them when they strolled past.

People here were eerily friendly, Madeline thought. Ciaran didn't look around much. He strode straight in as if he knew what to expect. The door closed behind them after they entered the hall.

Along the corridor, many people were milling about and talking animatedly as if they were at the intermission of a concert. They all looked oddly human. In this place, Madeline expected to be attacked by weird creatures rather than standing here watching fellow human beings interacting in a civilized manner. She couldn't quite catch the language they were using to communicate.

A door at the far end of the corridor opened.

They entered a grand reception room with a raised platform, where a beautiful White Queen sat on her icy white throne. Around the room were others who looked like servants, counsellors, and other authoritative figures.

Madeline noted that even Ciaran did not know the appropriate greeting etiquette. When the queen stood up and gave them a warm smile, he merely smiled back.

"Welcome to my humble residence," said the queen in a throaty and mysterious voice.

"Holy smoke, she spoke English," Tadgh muttered.

"You think she should speak French?" Zach asked.

"I'm not talking about the language. It's her tone. She sounds human. But she doesn't have any emotions. Not that I can tell."

"She might be robotic," Ciaran agreed.

The queen smiled. "Before we go any further, I'd like to let you know, I can hear what everyone says in this castle."

Madeline wanted to roll her eyes internally but resisted from doing so as she wasn't sure what game they were playing and whether the queen could read her thoughts.

The queen reached her hand out. Ciaran kissed it. "Thank you for having us."

The queen smiled graciously, "I love having you here. But I'm sure you don't want to remain residents here forever. It's best if you remain passing travelers."

Ciaran nodded. "Understood, White Queen."

The queen put on a bright smile. "Rumor has it that the King-to-be of Eudaiz is knowledgeable. You certainly do not disappoint, Ciaran."

"I wish the previous stage had been as hospitable as this one. My friends are tired. What do we have to do to obtain a pass through this stage?"

The queen laughed. "The Black stage is not meant to be friendly because you'd die if you didn't pass. We are friendly because we don't know who may end up being a permanent resident here."

"What are the odds?" Tadgh asked.

The queen smiled again. "This must be Tadgh, the last minute passenger. I can give you that information. No king successor has ever failed this stage. For others, however, eight out of ten fail. We can accommodate many as you can see." She gestured widely toward the people in the room.

"There are jobs and plenty of activities for you here. But you can't compare this place with Eudaiz. This is not a universe. It's just a humble institution," she finished with a smile.

"So at which stage would a king successor normally fail?" Madeline asked.

The queen cast a warm gaze on Madeline. "I know what you must be feeling, Madeline. But I can't give you that information."

"You are not serving the king?" Ciaran asked.

"Correct. Daimon Gate is a gateway to multiple universes. Not just Eudaiz. We manage and legitimize leaders of universes. Depending on the constitution and the setup of the universe, the test requirements will always be different."

"But you must have a leader?"

"Yes, we are governed by the Host and the council of the Daimon Gate. If you are successful to the kingship of Eudaiz, you might be dealing with them directly in the future."

"Can we meet them when we are passing this time?"

"Yes, but only if you win an invitation. No one has won it in the past."

"How can I get an invitation?"

"That information will be revealed after you have passed the next stage."

Ciaran nodded.

"Now, would you like to proceed through this stage as a group or as individuals?" the queen asked.

"I'd prefer as a group, and I'm happy to take the bulk of the tasks. But it's up to the individuals," Ciaran said.

"I'm in with Ciaran," Madeline said.

"Same," Tadgh said.

Zach contemplated, and then he nodded. "I'm in with the group."

The queen smiled. "Your group is quite cohesive. So hang on tight. And good luck." She turned on her heel and headed toward an endless corridor of white marble.

CHAPTER 23

They entered a square room with a wall-sized computer, similar to the one at the villa outside London. The air in the room hummed with the sound of technology. It felt as though ants were crawling on their skin with the computer eyes everywhere, watching their every move.

The queen entered a command into the control panel then turned around.

"This is not a computer-simulated game. This is the reality in Eudaiz at the moment. Each decision you make here will be executed later after you pass the Daimon Gate and take your respective roles in

Eudaiz. The decisions cannot be undone. You will get a green light for an optimal decision and move on. A red light will indicate a suboptimal decision. You are allowed only one suboptimal decision. There is no time restriction. Stay as long as you like. Questions?"

"What's next?" Ciaran asked.

"If you pass, the whole group will progress to the next stage. If you fail, you will all remain here until the end of your natural lives."

The queen left the room.

Ciaran shifted his still not perfect left shoulder and pressed his palm onto the control panel for print verification.

After the welcome message, text flew across the screen like breaking news:

The Black Rock is attacking District Five again and has killed several residents.

The death toll is not available at this stage.

Sciphil Five - Juliette Dubois has taken no action.

The district has received help from Sciphil Two - Ayana Dee and Sciphil Nine - Pete Chandler.

"We know why Juliette isn't taking action, you idiot," Tadgh mumbled.

Action needed. Choose one of the two solutions below.

One: Elimination by force.

Probability of success: Sixty percent.

Costs: One tower, one Sciphil, and two hundred thousand fighters.

Record: Attempted by Sciphil One - Richard Kelly.

Result: Failed.

Two: Building alliance with Earth.

Probability of success: Ten percent.

Costs: Compromised technology, risks of chemical contamination.

Record: Attempted by Kyle Wolf.

Result: Failed.

What is your chosen action: . . .

"That sucks," Zach said. "Surely there are other solutions."

Kyle preferred building alliances. That explained his actions and why he had ended up on Earth. Apparently, the fact that he attempted to build an alliance with the Black Rock was not on record,

Ciaran mused. He considered the information interesting. This step was a no-brainer for him.

"We'll go for war. I can do better with the second action than Kyle Wolf. But based on this record, number one is a more optimal solution," Ciaran said and entered: One.

The green light flashed.

The second lot of text appeared:

Earth attack.

A foreign chemical was introduced into Eudaiz's food supply system.

The chemical had been contained and terminated by Sciphil Three - Bran LeBlanc.

This is classified as an unprovoked attack from Earth.

Action needed. Choose one of the two solutions below.

One: Elimination by force.

Probability of success: Ninety percent.

Costs: Five hundred thousand fighters.

Record: Proposed by Sciphil Seven - Ralph Durant.

Result: Not yet attempted.

Two: Elimination of the source of the chemical on Earth. Target - the United Kingdom.
Probability of success: One hundred percent.
Costs: Ten specialists, one viral seed.
Record: Proposed by Sciphil Eight - Aiden Felix.
Result: Not yet attempted.

What is your chosen action?

"They are talking about sending a virus bomb to the UK. We all know where the attack on their food supply system came from. How could their records be so primitive?" Ciaran said.

"I don't know anything about the attack on their food supply system," Zach said.

"We have to go with number one. We can deal with fighters. But the viral bomb will be mass destruction," Ciaran said.

"You're having a conflict of interest, Ciaran. Who is fighting whom here?" Madeline said.

"I know. But do you have a better suggestion, Madeline?"

"In the best interest of Eudaiz, number two is the clear winner. But, as with Ciaran, I have a conflict of interest, so I wouldn't choose number two," Tadgh said.

"If we choose number one, it's going to be a red light," Madeline said.

Ciaran said nothing. He paced, contemplating.

"We have to follow through with one of the solutions. I can manage and control the fighters. The viral bomb, once executed, cannot be reversed, and the effects will be unpredictable," Ciaran said.

"How can five hundred thousand fighters take over the entire Earth?" Zach asked.

"That's why it's clearly an inferior decision for Eudaiz," Madeline said.

"I'd like to take the red light on this and do my best to green light the rest. What do you think?" Ciaran asked.

Tadgh said without hesitation, "I'm in."

"Me, too," Madeline said. She trusted her instincts and Ciaran's capability.

Zach contemplated, then he shrugged. "I'd prefer number two. But I'm outvoted. So take the red light then."

Ciaran entered: One.

The red light flashed.

Air supply shortage.
Eudaiz's air production system has been damaged by the Black Rock in the latest attack.

Air shortage occurred in District Nine and District One.

Action needed. Choose one of the two solutions below.
One: Trade with the Green Stars.
Probability of success: Ninety percent.
Costs: Seed energy of five hundred years supply for one hundred years of air supply.
Record: Proposed by Sciphil Nine - Pete Chandler.
Result: Not yet attempted.

Two: Steal from the Black Rock's natural air supply.
Probability of success: Ninety percent.
Costs: Two hundred fighters for a one-year air supply.
Record: Proposed by Sciphil One - Richard Kelley.
Result: Not yet attempted.

What is your chosen action?

"I am in for the trade with the Green Stars, solution one. Although stealing from the Black Rock is tempting, it can't be a long-term solution. Any objections?" Ciaran asked.

Everyone agreed on this scenario. Ciaran typed in one. The green light flashed.

More text flashed on the screen:

Sciphil successors and new appointments.

Due to the latest development in the council, changes need to be made to replace Sciphils and appoint new successors.

Action needed. Choose one of the four combinations below.

One:

Sciphil Three - Bran LeBlanc - replaced by Ciaran LeBlanc.

Sciphil One - Richard Kelley - replaced by Madeline Kelley.

Sciphil Two - Ayana Dee - successor appointed: Zach Flynn.

Sciphil Nine - Pete Chandler - successor appointed: Tadgh LeBlanc.

Termination: Sciphil Four - Kyle Wolf - replaced by George LeBlanc.

Termination: Sciphil Five - Juliette Dubois - replaced by Chloe Matheson.

Two:

Sciphil Three - Bran LeBlanc - replaced by Ciaran LeBlanc.

Sciphil One - Richard Kelley - replaced by Madeline Kelley.

Sciphil Two - Ayana Dee - successor appointed: Zach Flynn.

Sciphil Nine - Pete Chandler - successor appointed: Tadgh LeBlanc.

Termination: Sciphil Four - Kyle Wolf - replaced by Josephine Cassidy.

Termination: Sciphil Five - Juliette Dubois - replaced by George LeBlanc.

Three:

Sciphil Three - Bran LeBlanc - replaced by Ciaran LeBlanc.

Sciphil One - Richard Kelley - replaced by Madeline Kelley.

Sciphil Two - Ayana Dee - successor appointed: Zach Flynn.

Sciphil Nine - Pete Chandler - successor appointed: Tadgh LeBlanc.

Termination: Sciphil Four - Kyle Wolf - replaced by George LeBlanc.

Termination: Sciphil Five - Juliette Dubois - replaced by Daniel Chandler.

Four

Sciphil Three - Bran LeBlanc - replaced by Ciaran LeBlanc.

Sciphil One - Richard Kelley - replaced by Madeline Kelley.

Sciphil Two - Ayana Dee - successor appointed: Zach Flynn.

Sciphil Nine - Pete Chandler - successor appointed: Tadgh LeBlanc.

Termination: Sciphil Four - Kyle Wolf - replaced by Chloe Matheson.

Termination: Sciphil Five - Juliette Dubois - replaced by Josephine Cassidy.

What is your chosen action?

Ciaran found himself pacing back and forth in the room. There was no easy answer for this one, and they didn't have any red light allowance left.

CHAPTER 24

"The first four combinations are the same across the four scenarios. The differences are in the replacements for Kyle and Juliette," Ciaran said, more to himself than to others.

"Josephine Cassidy. Is that our Jo, Madeline?" Tadgh asked.

Madeline nodded.

"What does Chloe have to do with any of this? She doesn't even know about the Daimon Gate." Zach was astonished.

"You never know . . . she might have a hidden talent the multiverse needs." Ciaran smiled. "We know George. He helped design the lights to kill Juliette. He'd make an excellent Sciphil. We don't know Daniel Chandler," Ciaran said.

"It might be my buddy, Dan. But it might be just a person with the same name," Zach said.

"Who's he?" Madeline asked.

"He's Chloe's stepfather's son if that makes any sense. They moved to Australia a few years ago from England. He likes supernatural stuff. He's the one who worked out that Kyle Wolf was using the Zodiac system, and he saved my ass in a Japanese maze. But apart from being a pain in the neck, I don't know what his talent might be."

"Sounds as if he could be a candidate," Madeline said.

"They wouldn't just draw these names out of a hat," Tadgh said.

"I speculate that Daniel Chandler was put forward by Pete Chandler. Jo's there because of her relationship with Madeline. Chloe is there because of Zach. And George? It's obvious—he's a LeBlanc," Ciaran said.

"We have to keep in mind that the combination has to be in Eudaiz's best interest," Madeline said. "George is excellent. However, his name will add another LeBlanc to the council of nine Sciphils."

Ciaran nodded. "It would be three out of nine from the LeBlancs."

"Then Dan would add another Chandler—if they're really related. If the LeBlancs don't increase and the Chandlers do, we'd have the same voting power from both families. I can't imagine that's in the best interest of Eudaiz. We shouldn't take Dan if we don't take George," Zach said.

"It's best to have a clear dominant power, which is the LeBlancs. Then the rest should be equal. Because if we have the best and the second best, factions will occur," Tadgh said.

Ciaran smiled. He was pleased to see that Tadgh had matured a lot in the last few weeks. "Based on this analysis, it seems scenario four is the winner. However, there is one other thing to consider," Ciaran said.

"Which is?" Tadgh asked.

"We don't know what the best interest of Eudaiz *is*. We don't know the thought process behind this test. The balance of power is a natural and logical analysis from our perspective. But it might not be the most important issue for Eudaiz. If we look at the selection from a capabilities point of view instead of a power balance point of view, then George is an outstanding candidate."

"I have a good feeling about Daniel, too, although I haven't met him," Madeline said.

"Chloe is clearly not equipped for this at all," Zach said.

"Jo is excellent, but she is now with Kyle Wolf, and we don't know what will happen," Tadgh said.

Ciaran looked at Tadgh. He was glad Tadgh had voiced the reality about Jo. She could be dead, or she could have turned to the dark side with Kyle Wolf.

"I don't believe that the test program would have the information about Jo being with Kyle. But if it does, choosing Jo would be the worse decision," Ciaran said.

"If we can't choose Jo, then scenarios two and four are out," Madeline confirmed.

"We can't get this wrong," Zach stressed.

"Let's just figure this out with logic first. Between capability and the balance of power, which is best for Eudaiz? I'm saying it's capability," Ciaran said.

"Balance of power," Tadgh said.

"Same," Zach said.

"Capability," Madeline said.

Ciaran shook his head. "Two and two. This doesn't help at all. Your grandfather said your sixth sense is your talent. What is it saying at the moment, Madeline?"

"I told you—it's capability."

Ciaran nodded. "Okay. I'm pulling my leader's weight. We're going for capability. Based on that, I'm voting for George. That leaves us three scenarios left to work with—one, two, and three."

Ciaran hoped his decision was right, and he wasn't biased toward George because he was one of the LeBlancs. He had a lot of confidence in George. Although they didn't always agree on different issues, having a brain like George's in any committee was always a treasure. They had done enough business together for Ciaran to know this.

"Between Chloe and Daniel, I'd go for Daniel. Is that a fair choice, Zach?"

Zach nodded.

"Then number one is out of the picture," Tadgh said. "We don't know Daniel. But given Jo's situation at the moment, I'd go with him."

"Same with me," Madeline said.

"Dan is a good selection. You'll know it when you meet him," Zach said. "Jo is brilliant. But the Zodiac—I mean, Kyle—is evil. We don't know if we'll ever see the same Jo again."

Ciaran nodded. "We agree on number three then? George and Daniel?"

Everyone nodded. Ciaran entered three into the computer.

One minute passed.

Two minutes passed.

The monitor flashed a red light.

They couldn't believe their eyes. The red light blinked, mocking them.

Ciaran shook his head. "I'm sorry. I'm so sorry."

Tadgh touched his shoulder. "Don't worry, Ciaran. We're in this together. It's not your fault. I'm sure we'll grow to love life here in this ice haven."

Zach sat on the floor, leaning against the wall. "I hope they like my music here."

Madeline hugged Ciaran and gave him a kiss. "As long as we're together, I don't care where we live."

The door slid open and the queen sauntered in. The same smile was still on her face. "Well, we have accommodations to suit your tastes and keep you comfortable."

She approached Ciaran. "It's an honor to have the LeBlancs in residence. You may call me your White Queen now."

She reached out her hand for Ciaran to kiss.

Ciaran bent down and held her hand to kiss. Then he suddenly pulled her toward him, grabbed a dagger with his other hand, and pressed the blade against her neck.

"I've never before used a woman as a shield, but we can't stay here. The computer did not say we failed. We must have another chance. What was the right answer?" Ciaran asked.

"If I was scared of your weapons, do you think I'd let you carry them around in my castle?" the queen asked.

"I don't care. We have to pass. We get out of here, and you live. Otherwise, I'll slit your throat. I will get my people out of here at the very least."

Ciaran pressed the dagger harder against the queen's throat. A stream of blood ran down her neck and onto her white dress.

"I'll ask you one last time, what is the right answer?"

"Three."

"That's what we entered, bitch! Why did we get the red light?" Tadgh said.

The queen looked puzzled. She stuttered.

"She didn't even check our results!" Zach gasped.

"She wanted us to stay here. She faked the computer's response," Madeline said.

"I'm going to have a word with your Host," Ciaran told her.

The queen exhaled and whirled around at an incredible speed. The motion spun Ciaran out and into a wall.

"You won't make it out of here. You are mine," she said threateningly.

The queen stopped spinning and charged at Ciaran. He stood up quickly and swung his two daggers. There was a scream, and the queen vanished into a wall.

Footsteps shook the castle. Bloodcurdling screams were everywhere. Hellhounds howled and white ravens squawked. White bats flooded in from the outside.

The ice castle began to collapse. The white walls, pillars, and ceiling gave way. The floor beneath them shifted and broke apart into chunks of ice. They were standing on a huge raft of ice on a dark river.

Ciaran had seen this before in his subconscious. The dark water was underneath. Once they got below the surface, he would not be able to break the ice himself to come back up.

The floor tilted toward the water. It was so slippery.

"Don't fall into the water!" Ciaran called out to Tadgh and Zach, who were hanging onto the edge of the ice at the other end of the room.

The walls of the room caved in. They heard the roar of water from a waterfall. But there was no waterfall in the castle. It was the water from the melting snow splashing between the walls and the corridors.

They were on the verge of moving from stage two to stage three, Ciaran thought. He screamed over the top of the noise. "We are moving into stage three—the Red stage. This is a spiritual stage. We are looking for the sign of a phoenix to pass to stage three. Stay true to yourself . . ."

A gigantic wave of ice water poured into the room and wiped away everything and everyone.

Ciaran held tight to Madeline's hands for as long as he could, but under the icy water, everything went numb. He didn't know when she slipped out of his hands. He didn't know how many times he hit the ice rocks.

It was dark. Ciaran couldn't see Madeline, Tadgh, or Zach anymore.

CHAPTER 25

Madeline woke in a cold stone room. She sat up and tried to gather her bearings. It was a round room that looked like a tower. Medieval-style torches hung on the walls, shedding enough light for her to see the door and figure out that she was locked inside.

A tiny and useless window was located near the ceiling. She couldn't even tell whether it was day or night by looking at it. She couldn't be in another castle, could she? If she ever got back to New York, she swore she would never visit another castle again.

Madeline couldn't remember much except for the cold water and rocks of ice that kept hitting her. She remembered the dark water and Ciaran's hand slipping away from hers.

Where was everyone?

A white dove landed at the hole she called a window. It cooed.

Madeline smiled. "Got something for me?" She couldn't believe her eyes when the bird flew in and landed on the floor next to her. There was a note attached to its leg.

"You've got to be kidding me." She took the note.

"Coming in to get you. Hang in there. Tadgh & Zach."

But where was Ciaran? What did it mean? She would hang on. There wasn't much else she could do. She tried to recall what Ciaran had said about this stage and plan for what might lie ahead.

This was a stage made more for Ciaran than anyone else. It was a stage for the king to prove he was purified and consummated with his queen. It was a stage of rebirth. Also, it was a very sexual stage, whatever that meant.

Was she his queen?

What if he consummated with the wrong queen?

She wouldn't mind if he had to have sex with someone as a requirement for this stage. But consummation was far more than having sex as far as she was concerned. It was a sexual act between *soul mates*. It required love.

Damn! She sounded more and more like Ciaran by the second.

She didn't want to think anymore.

Madeline bit her finger for some blood and wrote on the note. "Will make it out. Wait." She tied the note to the dove's foot. "How cinematic," she grumbled to herself. "The next thing I'll see is a dark prince in this black castle."

As soon as the bird left the room, she heard footsteps. The heavy door slid open, revealing a magnificent dark prince. She glanced around to see if there was a computer in this room, reading her thoughts and conveying them to the hologame designer.

This wasn't a hologame. But it wasn't real, either.

Madeline swore to God that this prince existed only in fairy tales. He had an aura that could stir every woman on Earth's loins. Madeline shook her head to clear it.

First, she was not on Earth. She was sure of it. Second, if she was a little stirred up because of the personification of sexual magnetism standing in front of her, she was sure every other woman would be, too. She was no exception, and it was not an act of infidelity. Third, infidelity only applied to married couples or people who had made vows. Ciaran and she had yet to make any promises to each other. And fourth—

"You look pleased. I wager you like the idea," the prince said.

"Huh?"

"I asked if you'd care to join me for dinner."

"Okay." Madeline glanced at the window. No bird. No message.

"Where am I?"

"The Red Castle."

"Are you the king?"

He laughed. "No, I'm the prince of this castle. We do not have a king."

The prince placed his arm supportively around her waist and led her to a long corridor lined with guards.

She was sure there were real people hidden beneath the lifeless steel armor. This felt a little like Lumley Castle. The difference was that instead of having Ciaran, she had a dark prince. It may have suited her teenage fantasies, but it did not suit her now. She knew what she had to do.

They entered a large medieval hall. A long dining table was covered with a feast large enough to feed all of the inhabitants of New York. She sat opposite the prince. He raised a pewter goblet to her. Madeline guessed that it held wine. She did the same.

"How did I get here?" Madeline asked.

"God brought you to me."

In her mind, Madeline rolled her eyes. "I understand. But how exactly did you find me?"

"You were washed onto the shore from the White Castle. That was a nasty one, wasn't it?"

"Were there other people with me?"

"We found you and Ciaran. My sister is taking care of him. He is doing fine."

The statement assaulted her brain like a cannonball. His sister was taking care of Ciaran? In front of her was a prince, and that made his sister a princess. And she was now caring for the King-to-be of Eudaiz. *What would a princess do to become a queen?* Madeline heard herself snarling inside. *Sexual stage, my ass!*

She pasted a gracious smile on her face and looked at the prince.

"You knew we were coming?" That was such a rhetorical question, Madeline thought.

"Yes. We received information about your arrival. You, Ciaran, and the two monkeys in the bush."

"Two monkeys?"

"Tadgh and Zach, right? They ran into the bush as soon as they landed.

Madeline nodded. "So we're friends. We're your guests, right?"

"Of course. We receive travelers now and then who pass through the Daimon Gate. You want me to send for your other two friends?"

Madeline nodded. The prince sipped his wine and signaled his guards to retrieve Zach and Tadgh.

This is too easy. What are you up to? Madeline narrowed her eyes.

The prince gestured at the food. Madeline stabbed her fork into something that looked like either a very large grape or a relatively small tomato. The prince cut into a piece of grilled game bird. Madeline prayed it wasn't her messenger dove.

"Based on the information I received, Tadgh, Zach, and yourself have passed the Daimon Gate at an individual levels. The only person who has yet to go through the final transmutation process is Ciaran."

"You're saying that I am free to leave the Daimon Gate right now?

"Yes."

"What's the catch?"

"What do you mean?"

"It can't be that easy. What do you want from me?"

The prince smiled. "I wish my sister had a fraction of your knowledge."

"I wouldn't call it knowledge. It's life experience."

The prince nodded. "We haven't had many passengers from Eudaiz. It has been a while actually. We have many from other universes. My sister is fond of Ciaran. And I am fond of you."

Madeline raised an eyebrow. She did not like what she was thinking. This stage had obviously high sexual connotations.

The prince put his wine down. He moved toward Madeline's side of the table. He sat down next to her, using his finger to trace her jawline.

"This kind of beauty has never passed through my castle before. Are you married?"

Shit! She had been too busy to thinking about Ciaran and had totally forgotten that the sexual connotation thing applied to her as well. As long as she stayed here.

"No," she responded.

He nodded and smiled. "I'm the prince of this castle. I can give my wife a very good life. This may not compare with Eudaiz. But we have peace, and we can live a lavish life. I am not sure what more a woman could wish for."

If she could have banged her head on the table, she would have. If she said no, he wouldn't give her more information about Ciaran. If she said yes, hell, she didn't know what would happen after that.

She grabbed the steak knife and cut into something on her plate that looked like meat. She just wanted a weapon in her hands.

CHAPTER 26

It was a hell that was labeled as heaven. Ciaran found it amusing. It was so trashy that he wouldn't even put it in a game of the lowest caliber. He was walking through rows and rows of the most exotic and sexual displays possible. Everything imaginable was being offered to him.

All he needed to do was to take.

He strode along the corridor. The women surrounded him, enticing him. He pushed through to the door ahead. He'd nearly reached it when he felt a strong pull. He turned around.

The woman was Laurent, and she had tears in her eyes. She was the dearest friend of Juliette, the wife of his best friend. Her death was one of the deepest regrets in his life.

"Take me out of here. They locked me in here to entertain the guests. It's worse than hell. Please, Ciaran, take me with you. For old time's sake," she whispered.

Ciaran paused.

She reached her hand out.

He wanted save her. He felt obliged to take her with him. He owed her entire family his life. He couldn't leave her here in this brothel.

If there was one.

His mind clicked instantly. He was at the Red stage of the Daimon Gate test. He had to remember that. He scolded himself and turned away from the image of the woman.

He kept walking.

A bloodcurdling scream echoed behind him. He knew the creatures were torturing Laurent's image. He couldn't look back, or he would return to save her.

He kept walking.

More screams. More cries of his name. More begging.

Sounds of weapons slashing at bodies, claws tearing into flesh, and body parts being torn off.

Moaning, crying, cursing, and death wishes.

He'd prefer physical pain to this. But he put his head down, concentrated, and kept walking.

He reached his hand out to push the door open.

***

Madeline focused on her meal and ignored the prince's rants about the lavish life he could give her should she agree to be his wife. "I'm sure it's wonderful to live here." She grinned.

"Would you like to?"

"I'm designated to be a Sciphil. I made my promise."

The prince shook his head. "It's a pity. You'd make a good wife. You're not betrothed to Ciaran, are you?"

"Oh, no. There's no such thing in my world. Just out of curiosity, what does Ciaran have to do to pass this stage?" Madeline asked and mustered the most gracious smile she could.

"This is a spiritual stage. He must remain true to himself and be reborn by consummating with his queen."

Madeline knew this. It should be easy enough for her and Ciaran. Why should it be such a big deal? Why did the prince seem worried and doubtful?

"You think Ciaran won't pass? I saw concern in your eyes."

He smiled. "Thank you. It's very kind of you to notice. I'm worried about my sister. She wants to be a White Queen. She should have been one a long time ago. Given you have just killed a White Queen, this is a perfect opportunity for my sister. But I'm afraid she wants it too much. She might rush it. And Ciaran is too damaged to be good for her."

"What do you mean by that?"

"The man is spiritually damaged. I don't think he will pass this stage. He doesn't seem to have a spiritual belief. If she consummates with him, he might be the wrong king."

Madeline shifted in her chair. How about her being the wrong queen? "You said consummate. Exactly when did they get married?"

"That's what I'm worried about. She couldn't get him to say the words. You are his Sciphil, his counsellor. You must know him. Do you know a way?"

Madeline swallowed a laugh.

"A way to do what?"

"Help my sister."

"Help her make him say the words? You mean to marry her?"

"It's just a ritual. He asks her to be his queen. They consummate. That's all she needs. She could do it with any other leaders from any other universe. It doesn't have to be Eudaiz, and it doesn't have to be Ciaran. She's just stuck on him for some reason."

The prince looked genuinely concerned. Madeline took pity on him. She understood why his sister would not let go of Ciaran. That was the very reason he was hers. And she was going to make very sure it stayed that way. Her way.

"How was your sister trying to make Ciaran say the words, exactly? Knowing him, I couldn't think of anything that would scare him off easily."

"She didn't scare him. He was washed up on the shore with you. He had some injuries. She gave him something to soothe the physical pain—"

"She drugged Ciaran?" Madeline couldn't help but laugh.

"It wasn't a drug. It was an Inducer of the subconscious state of mind, where the spirit can be purified and transformed. She didn't know he would go down that deep, not wanting to resurface."

"You mean, he's in a coma?"

"Medically, it might look that way. But it is a spiritual transmutation process. It's not a coma. People choose the subconscious levels they want to go to and the level they want to come back to. Or to not come back to."

"So he didn't want to come back to your sister. Is that what you're saying?"

"Effectively, yes."

"If she really wants to be his true queen, shouldn't she be down in the subconscious levels looking for him? Wouldn't the whole deal of marriage and consummation involve a little thing called love?"

"Love?"

Madeline rolled her eyes. "Great. It's not even in your dictionary."

"If you mean that to have *love*, my sister has to go down there looking for him, then she couldn't do that. Spiritually, they're not connected. She might not be able to find him, and she might not be able to come back herself. It's dangerous down there."

The prince emphasized the word 'love' by stretching its pronunciation.

"What kind of danger?"

"It's a mind maze. The only right path is the path where you stay true to yourself. Any moment of doubt or faint waver in belief will send you in the wrong direction. Lost people will stay in oblivion forever. Those who pass this stage will have the highest level of consciousness."

Madeline manufactured a concerned look. "I can go down and find Ciaran for your sister. All you want is for him to return so he can marry your sister and have sex with her? Is that correct?"

"Such a vulgar term."

"That's essentially what she wants."

"You would do that? Go down and bring him back? Why?"

"We entered the Daimon Gate as a group, and we will leave as a group. That's what we call loyalty. I wager you don't have that term in your dictionary, either."

"Indeed, we don't. But it sounds intriguing."

The guards led Zach and Tadgh into the room. They glanced at the prince.

"We passed the Daimon Gate, guys, according to the prince," Madeline said before Tadgh and Zach speculated. "The only person who had to dive deep into this level was Ciaran, and he is currently still diving."

"But we—" Tadgh said.

"As friends," Madeline emphasized her pronunciation of friends and hoped Tadgh got the hint, "we promised to enter and leave this gate together. Ciaran is stuck somewhere in his subconscious, and I need to retrieve him."

"But how?" Zach said.

"Oh, they've done this before. They know what to do." Tadgh brushed it off.

"Really? You do this often?" the prince asked.

"This is routine on Earth," Madeline said, thinking about the nights Ciaran and she had spent together. "And the most important thing is that while I am down there, no one can interrupt us, including your sister. You don't want us to get lost, do you?"

"Of course not."

Zach stood puzzled.

Tadgh approached Madeline. "Let's get him out of here," he whispered.

The prince led the way to a chamber via a wide corridor. He knocked on the door and entered. Madeline, Tadgh, and Zach followed him inside.

On an enormous bed on a raised platform covered in velvet, Ciaran lay sleeping. Next to the bed stood a beautiful mermaid walking on two legs. Her dreamy blue eyes were filled with tears. She ran toward the prince.

"Brother, he wouldn't wake. I can't wake him. I might have killed him."

Zach shifted at the statement. Tadgh whispered very softly to him, "He's like that with sedatives. He won't wake up." Zach didn't nod but stopped shifting and showed signs of agitation.

"I brought you these warriors. They are his friends. They will help him return, my princess," the prince said.

Madeline spoke between her teeth to Zach and Tadgh. "Hooray, we've been promoted to warrior status."

"Really? What do you need? Tell me what to do," the mermaid princess said to Madeline.

"Just give me what you gave him and then leave us alone. Don't come in until we call you. Understood?" Madeline said.

The princess didn't seem to understand. The prince grabbed the drug, gave it to Madeline, and took the princess out of the room.

Madeline went to the bed and looked at Ciaran sleeping peacefully. Then she looked at the drug. "I'm going down with him. I think this is the same as the training he had before."

"That's purely speculation, Madeline. We don't have any support here. No Doctor Thomas, no Jo, no George. What do you suggest we do if you don't come back up? Pick you both up and run away?" Tadgh asked.

"Can you brief me on the plans, please, whatever they might be?" Zach asked.

"Whenever Ciaran is in a comatose state, he generally can't come out of it quickly or without assistance. Last time, I had to go in and yank him out," Madeline said.

Zach's jaw dropped.

"What if it doesn't work this time?" Tadgh asked.

"I don't have any other solutions. Do you?"

Silence.

"Guess not. So please guard us, and don't let these people near us. I'll see what I can do."

Tadgh nodded.

"Zach?"

"Okay. Sure." Zach nodded.

Madeline quickly got onto the bed. She kissed Ciaran. No response. She took the drug and lay down next to him.

CHAPTER 27

The room greeted Ciaran with a blast of light. A web of tangled robes flew at him. Before he could react, he was tied up, arms and legs stretched toward four corners of the room. *Torture chamber?* he wondered.

The door swung open, and a group of women sauntered in. Their beauty exceeded all standards across the cosmos. Sexuality oozed from every pore of their skin.

"Coming down here without a chosen queen, Ciaran? Let us help you," one of them said. He didn't know which one it was as he kept his eyes closed.

He had yanked at the rope many times and had given up the idea that he could break himself loose.

They could tie him up, but they couldn't force him to open his eyes. Thus, their beauty wasn't working as effectively as it might. He knew if he gave in to the pleasure, he would have to choose a queen right here. If it was the wrong queen, it would lead to death. If it was the right queen, then he would consummate.

As to what constituted a right or wrong choice, he had no clue. His knowledge of alchemy wasn't that extensive.

He could hear the women peeling their clothes off. He heard them whispering about what would trigger sexual urges. That, he could handle easily. He just ignored what they said.

"Why don't we take turns? Then all you have to do is say which one of us you like best," a voice suggested.

Then he felt their hands all over him. They knew how to physically work a man to get what they wanted. He was only human. He knew that. Regardless of how strong his mental capacity was, he knew these women—or creatures—would work him until they got what they needed.

He could let it get to that point.

Creatures?

Yes! They were creatures! Not humans. Not women.

"I will not choose any of you. Don't waste your time," he said.

"Oh, you can't be so sure."

"Get off me, or you will regret it. I've given you fair warning."

"We only want to pleasure you."

They were all over him again.

"Last warning. Get off me."

They kept coming.

"You've forced me to do this," he growled and wielded the blade in his mind.

And his fury came forth. He could feel the force of the blade spinning in the room. It slashed, stabbed, cut, and tore at anything in its flying path.

He opened his eyes and saw body parts, blood, and flesh raining down on him.

The ropes were cut.

He freed himself and stood up, tucking his weapons in place.

On the floor, what looked like might have been human body parts had turned into robotic parts. The blood had changed into an oily black liquid which had pooled on the floor and now evaporated into thin air.

Ciaran stepped around the room, avoiding the puddles, and approached the door to the next room. As he pushed the door open, the room exploded with colors and shapes which flew directly at him.

CHAPTER 28

Madeline drifted down. And down. She swam in a dark space. Then she landed on firm ground inside a very plain chapel. The place looked familiar—long hall, arched pillars, and altar at the far end.

She approached a door, the only door in the room, and pushed it open.

She was immediately pulled into the room and surrounded by several *Madelines*. The door slammed behind her—there was no way out.

At the other end of the room stood Ciaran, covered in blood, gripping his daggers. He looked at her like she was a stranger.

Hundreds of creatures in the room in female form flew at him. He slaughtered them before they touched him. But that wasn't the problem.

She could see the deadly problem.

There were hundreds of creature taking her likeness. They looked identical to her. They approached Ciaran slowly in small groups. When they got close, and if he didn't kill them, they clawed at him. That explained why he was covered in blood.

He slashed at most of them with his daggers. There must be something in them that made him realize they weren't her. But he let a few slip too close before he killed them.

Even she couldn't tell the difference between herself and the row of creatures standing next to her right now, waiting for their turn to approach Ciaran.

She could attack them now and kill them, and then Ciaran would be able to tell it was her. She grabbed her daggers but realized they were no longer with her.

No weapons for Madeline.

She could see Ciaran grow angrier as more and more Madeline lookalikes clawed at him and bit him. He began to slash at them indiscriminately.

She knew he would get to a point where he sent out the blade of fury from his mind, and that would kill all creatures in the room—including her.

Doing that meant he would kill his true queen and lose this round of the test. But if he didn't do something, they would eat him alive. It was already starting to look like that was going to happen.

Madeline left the row of pretenders and started to approach Ciaran, like the other look-alike. She focused and tried to connect with his mind.

She knew it wouldn't work. But she had to try.

"Ciaran! It's me!" she called out to him in her mind.

No reaction from him. He kept stabbing and slashing at the lookalikes. Hundreds of Madelines.

Their attacks grew fiercer as they got closer. He slaughtered harder and harder.

A chill ran up her spine when she looked into his eyes.

He had grown used to slaughtering her image. The more he killed, the fewer injuries he had to suffer.

She approached him. Closer. Closer.

She had nothing with which to defend herself. Her psychic connection to him wasn't working.

All she had was herself and her love for him. She came even closer. So close she could smell the violence coming from him in waves.

He swung his daggers left, right, and in all directions. The bodies of her lookalikes fell like tree trunks to the floor.

He didn't even look to see if they evaporated or lay on the floor in a heap of blood, flesh, and bones, meaning he had just killed the real Madeline.

He just slaughtered.

One creature after another.

She approached. It was now her turn. She stood right in front of him.

She saw a dagger swing at her, aimed at her chest. He was going to stab her in the heart.

She did nothing. She just looked at him.

Then the dagger stopped right in front of her. The sharp point of the blade had sneaked into her flesh and cut loose a drop of blood.

Ciaran looked into her eyes.

"It's you!" he whispered in disbelief. "My queen." He dropped the daggers and pulled her into his arms. He squeezed her so hard it knocked the breath out of her.

He didn't care what was happening around him. If this was the wrong choice, if she was a creature, she could have turned around and ripped out his throat.

He didn't seem to care. His body vibrated with emotion. He buried his head in the crook of her neck. The he lifted her face up and kissed her.

And then it was her turn to not care what was happening around them in the room.

When the best kiss in the cosmos had finished, Ciaran released her. They looked around the room and saw that all the creatures—dead and alive—had vanished.

He had made the right choice.

He held her hand and led her to the next room where she had seen the altar before.

The room was now lit up with thousands of candles. Soft ceremonial music chanted from somewhere in the air. He looked at her.

His face, the face of a dark angel, was looking at her with love. She would trade anything to remain in that world and hold that look for the rest of her life.

They kissed again.

After a while, he asked, "Can you ever forgive me for what I did to Juliette? Will it ever come between us?"

Madeline cupped his face and immersed herself in his intense gray eyes. "Juliette was a part of your life. You will always carry the guilt of her natural death. We can't forget that. But she has never—and *will* never—come between us."

He kissed her again.

"I killed an innocent man. Will you be able to live with that?"

Ciaran looked at her. He rubbed his thumb on the dimple on her left cheek. "You'll kill more men. Whether good or evil, innocent or guilty, you will make a just decision of whether a life is worth preserving. You have an important role right now. People depend on you. You don't have to ask me that anymore. I'll answer it, once and for all. I love you, and I respect your decisions. Nothing else matters."

Madeline smiled.

They held each other for a long moment, swaying with the flow of the air. They swam in pleasant thoughts and happiness. Madeline did not know that happiness flowed like a current. It had frequency and rhythm. When she paid attention and reached out for it, she could actually feel it.

In that quietness, they heard each other's heartbeats.

"Will you marry me?" Ciaran asked.

She looked him in the face so that he could see her eyes.

"Yes," she said.

There were no tears on her face, not even happy ones. She was entitled to this happiness. She loved him. At this moment, she made a vow to herself that she would do whatever it took to protect her happiness and the love they had for each other.

Ciaran took her to the altar where a fire was burning on a reddened stone.

"This is the eternal fire, the fire of purity."

Ciaran pulled out his dagger and rested the blade in the flame.

"By the fire of God, I, Ciaran LeBlanc, ask Madeline Kelley to be my soul mate. I ask her to be my wife. I am the Red King, and she is my Queen. I vow to love and protect her for the rest of my life."

He used the blade to cut a ring line around her ring finger. Then he gave her the dagger.

"By the fire of God, I, Madeline Kelley, vow to be Ciaran LeBlanc's soul mate. I vow to be his wife and take him as my husband. He is my Red King and I am his Queen. I vow to love and protect him for the rest of my life."

She cut a blood ring on his ring finger.

They were now husband and wife.

In the absolute quietness, surrounded by nothingness, at this astronomical moment, all the dust in their minds was wiped away, and love enlightened them.

Their experience was complete. They were one. They had unified.

They consummated their vows. Their bodies, their souls, and their life forces entwined into one perfect essence of purified love.

Then and there, they heard a cooing sound. They looked up and saw a magnificent phoenix flapping its wings, flying away.

"My Queen, I'm glad to announce that we have passed the Red stage and the Daimon Gate test," Ciaran said.

CHAPTER 29

Madeline resurfaced in the castle first. Tadgh and Zach darted to the bed.

"You got him?" Tadgh asked.

Madeline put on a smile Tadgh had never seen before.

"What's with the smile?" he asked.

She revealed the blood ring.

"Holy . . ."

Madeline gestured for silence. She kissed Ciaran and shook his shoulders. "Ciaran, darling. You need to get up."

Ciaran opened his eyes. He was groggy, but he registered the reality instantly. He grabbed Madeline's hand and kissed her blood ring finger.

"Thanks for sharing," Tadgh mumbled.

"Great stuff." Zach grinned.

Ciaran flew out of the bed and slumped to the floor, vomiting in the corner of the room.

Zach jumped aside. "What's the . . ."

"He does that all the time. Keep it in mind before you feed him sedatives," Tadgh told Zach.

The prince and the princess rushed into the room. The princess darted over to Ciaran. "Are you sick? I'm so sorry? The inducer was too strong."

Ciaran shrugged away from the princess's supportive arms and stood up. Madeline came over and stood next to Ciaran.

"Thank you for your hospitality. But I'm afraid that we have to leave now," Ciaran said.

"You don't remember me at all, do you?" The princess's eyes filled with tears.

"No, I don't. Please refresh my memory."

"She is the princess of this castle. She saved you when you were half dead on the beach," the prince said.

"We're supposed to get married." The princess started crying.

"I beg your pardon?" Ciaran nearly jumped out of his skin.

"You're supposed to marry me. You are the Red King, and I am your Queen. To pass the Red stage of the Daimon Gate, you have to connect with your Queen. I am she. How can you not remember?" the princess wailed.

Ciaran shifted. Madeline sensed his movements, and they stepped closer to the door where Tadgh and Zach were standing.

Ciaran held up Madeline's hand.

"This is my Queen. We have married and consummated. And we have passed the gate. I am sorry if there was anything I did that caused you to misconstrue my intentions. We are only passengers here. We are not supposed to engage with the gatekeepers."

The princess wailed more.

"Gatekeepers!" the prince growled. "You Eudaiz passengers. You used us. You were supposed to fight for the Inducer. A fight for your life. Very few pass it. But my sister just gave it to you. So you passed through the transmutation process the easy way and married another queen. What sort of king does that make you?"

"Had I known, I would have been more than happy to accept the challenges and fight for the

Inducer. I cannot reverse the process. What would you like me to do to repay you for your help?"

"Our help? Don't even say that word. It's going to cost us our heads," the prince roared.

The princess reeled and fainted to the floor. The prince raced to her side and held her up. "Oh, my poor trusting sister. I'm so sorry. I should have taught you better. I should have been a better brother."

Then he looked at Ciaran. "All her life, all she wanted was to be a White Queen. Many leaders from other universes have been through our gate, and she could have married any one of them. But she wouldn't. It had to be the future King of Eudaiz. It had to be you."

"Why?" Ciaran asked. He approached the prince. "Because you fed her with fairy tales about Eudaiz? You've been telling her about a perfect world that doesn't exist, have you?"

"Eudaiz doesn't exist?" The prince was astonished.

"It does. I've never been to it, but I am quite sure it's not a perfect world," Madeline said from the door.

"But Eudaiz is happiness. It means happiness. True happiness is perfect. What else would one would live for?"

Ciaran shook his head. "You're responsible for screening people's spiritual purity and their worthiness before they get the Inducer for the final transmutation process, am I correct?"

The prince nodded.

"What the princess did was the equivalent of cheating and smuggling people through the gate. Yes?"

A tear of fear made its way down the prince's face. He looked at Ciaran. "If you married her as planned, things would be different," he said. "I guess you're not going to do that."

"What's the punishment?"

"Death for me and for her. Sanction for the castle and my territory. We will have no more passengers. Everything will be cut off until the area dries out."

"If you knew this disastrous outcome was possible, why did you let her do this?"

"I didn't let her. I wasn't quick enough to stop her. I can't let her die in this castle. The Host can chop my head off or do whatever. But she's just a child."

"How would the Host find out about this?"

"He already knows. When you received the Inducer without going through the challenges, the system expected a marriage between you and the princess. You must have seen the Phoenix?"

Ciaran nodded.

"The Host has now been informed that the marriage was between you and a different queen and that my sister cheated the system. She's doomed."

"How can I fix this?"

The prince smiled bitterly. "There is no way to fix it. Although, as a first time passenger, you have a chance to take a challenge. If you win, you will receive an invitation to meet the Host—and a privilege. With the privilege, you can ask for a pardon for my princess."

"Then I shall take the challenge," Ciaran said dryly.

The prince shook his head. "I should give my congratulations. You passed the Daimon Gate. Your transport is waiting for you at the gate. This will be my last chance to take any passengers through this castle. Bon voyage."

The prince sat still on the floor, leaning against the wall and holding his sister in his arms.

"What's your name?" Ciaran asked.

"Brandon."

"Brandon, I'll find a way to help you and your sister. I promise," Ciaran said firmly and headed toward the door.

Ciaran, Madeline, Tadgh, and Zach left the Red Castle, but just before they did, Madeline's psychic mind kicked in. She heard a loud and clear thought. "You'll never pass the gate alive, Ciaran."

She looked around. She didn't know whose thought she'd heard. The princess was still out, and the prince was still crying and stunned by the consequences of what they had done.

CHAPTER 30

Four horses raced across a field of roses. Madeline had never seen so many wild roses in her life. Beautiful and mysterious. Ciaran, on his white horse, led the group like a true king. In her mind, he had always been more a warrior than a king.

She'd had no idea riding a horse for the first time in her life could be this easy and fun. Zach and Tadgh seemed to manage it easy enough also. They raced as fast as the wind.

Snow-topped mountains fenced in the valley, leading them to the magnificent opening of a canyon. There was no need for Ciaran to say a word—they all knew that in front of them was the way out of the Daimon Gate.

Ciaran turned around. "Ayana and Pete will be waiting for you outside the gate. I'll be right behind you."

"Did you forget something back at the Red Castle, Ciaran? I know the mermaid princess was hard to let go," Madeline said.

Ciaran smiled. "Yes, I forgot my four wives and the dozen children I created when we were in the gate."

Madeline rubbed at her tummy. "Well, that saves me from doing the hard labor."

"Seriously, man, what do you need to do?" Zach asked.

"I promised Bran I would get the invitation," Ciaran said.

"Promised? When?" Tadgh raised his voice.

"When he was trying to give me the training."

"You mean the subconscious training session that almost killed you? The one where I had to dive into the ice water and yank you out? The one where you were hooked to a TV screen and almost died in front of us?" Madeline's voice raised in pitch.

"Didn't the prince say that you have to take a hard challenge to get the invitation? It's not a freebee, Ciaran," Zach said.

"Why did you promise Bran?" Madeline asked.

"He promised to give me information about Mother."

"How do you know he wasn't bluffing? She might be out there, on Earth, looking for us," Tadgh said.

"Knowing that it might be a bluff, do you expect me to say no to Bran's offer, Tadgh?"

Tadgh shook his head.

"I can't do anything until you are all safely out of the gate. Off you go. Please." Ciaran gestured toward the opening.

"I'm married to you. I don't want to have to handle another wannabe queen lurking around. I'm staying," Madeline insisted.

"Yeah, too bad. I'm your brother. If I let you find Mother yourself, you'll bad-mouth me to her for the rest of my life. I can't let that happen. I'm staying, too." Tadgh rubbed the neck of his horse.

"You should go, Zach," Ciaran said.

"I don't have a reason to stay, but I'll stick around." Zach cast a careless look at Ciaran.

Ciaran's horse started to get agitated and stomp around. He patted it to calm it down.

"How do you give Bran the invitation? I assume he wants it," Tadgh asked.

"I have to find him."

"Right, so there's a finding-Bran stage after passing the challenges?" Madeline asked.

Ciaran nodded.

"And whatever the invitation allows you to do, do you have to do that for Bran, too?" Madeline continued her questioning.

Silence.

"That's a yes," Tadgh said.

Madeline got off her horse. Ciaran did the same. He approached her. "I'll also get a privilege with the invitation. And I need to give that to the princess if you don't mind."

"I don't mind. Why would I? But the challenge bothers me."

"It's not hard."

"Tadgh, Ciaran said the challenges aren't hard!" Madeline pointed at Ciaran.

Tadgh got off his horse. "He's right. Just a bunch of snow-mummies, a pack of wolves, a burning forest, a collapsing bridge over a canyon, and ice water. Piece of cake."

"All right, okay. What do you want me to do?" Ciaran asked.

"Well, I'm not going to sit here and wait. I want in—all the way. I'm going in with you," Madeline said.

"Same here," Tadgh said dryly.

"I—"

"You don't think I'm useless, do you?" Zach asked.

"You saw the training, you two. You can tell Zach how dangerous it was."

Zach shifted his shoulders. "I'll do my best. What does the invitation look like?"

"Do I have a choice?" Ciaran looked at Tadgh, Madeline, and Zach. They glanced at him and waited for him to answer his own rhetorical question.

"Very well. Let's go," Ciaran muttered. He hopped on his horse. "This is a hybrid game between augmented reality and a hologame. We will play the scenarios as we go. Death and injuries during the game will have realistic impacts. But I don't know their extent. The invitation and the privilege will be placed in a box. That's all I know."

Zach rolled his eyes. "Well, how insightful."

Tadgh laughed.

"Let's go." Ciaran's horse wanted to do just that. It raced across the hill of wild roses. The other three horses lagged behind but caught up quickly.

They arrived at a meadow. Madeline remembered it. They had seen it before in Ciaran's training.

"We'll start here," Ciaran said.

"We have company," Madeline said. "Kyle is here."

CHAPTER 31

Tadgh said nothing. He glanced off into the distance and felt a tingle in his heart when he saw Jo riding alongside Kyle, both of them on black horses. Tadgh shook his head and tried to see Jo's emotions. He saw nothing. This Daimon Gate had somehow blocked his newfound ability. He cursed silently.

Jo was alive. That was all that mattered.

She was in black leather attire, double swords suspended from her back. Her hair blew back as she rode, making the angles of her foxy face sharper.

Her green eyes shone brilliantly. They smiled at Tadgh.

Kyle and Jo approached but slowed and stopped at a distance. Jo looked at Tadgh and nodded slightly.

"I hope we are not in competition here, Ciaran," Kyle said.

"I think we are," Ciaran responded dryly.

Ciaran's white horse and Kyle's black horse stepped back and forth, stomping their front hooves in agitation.

"I need only the privilege. If you're after the invitation, then we are not in competition."

"The invitation and the privilege come together. I have promised the privilege to someone. I'll need both the invitation and the privilege," Ciaran said.

"The privilege is for Jo, not for me. I dragged her into the gate against her will. I thought I could appoint her as a Sciphil. Turns out that I can't because I've been exiled. Jo needs a pardon from the Host. She needs the privilege."

"Otherwise?" Ciaran asked.

"Death by a thousand lightning bolts at the exit. Is that what you want for her?"

Everyone looked at Jo. Her face was as cool as steel. She kept her eyes on Tadgh.

Ciaran turned around, looking at Madeline. She showed neither approval nor rejection. That was enough for Ciaran. That meant she couldn't read anything from Jo.

Ciaran nodded. "Fine. If you honor what you say, we can benefit from the collaboration. If you don't, there may be a long future ahead for us, but I promise to cut yours short."

Kyle nodded.

They raced ahead along the meadow. Ciaran and Kyle led the group. Jo managed to pull her horse up to ride next to Tadgh. She looked at him again. This time, she smiled. That was Jo's smile. Tadgh was sure of it.

"I thought we lost you," Tadgh said.

Jo said nothing. She reached over and stuck a black rose next to Tadgh's daggers. She smiled again. Tadgh grinned and pushed his horse to get closer to her. But she pushed ahead and rode alongside Kyle.

In front of them, an army of faceless mummies rose from the tall grass. The mummies formed a line across the meadow and charged at them. This was the exact scenario from Ciaran's subconscious training.

The group charged straight ahead, six warriors on horseback. With weapons drawn and eyes fierce, they were ready to kill.

"Round them up," Ciaran said.

The horses ran in a circle, surrounding the mummies who hurled stones at them. Speed helped. They had horses and thus had the advantage.

Kyle and Jo had long, black spears. Ciaran, Madeline, Tadgh, and Zach had two daggers each. They rounded up the mummies, killing a number of them without much difficulty. The rest ran away, howling like wounded dogs.

"Fire is coming. Go left," Ciaran said.

The group veered left and raced toward the cliff. They had seen this before. A skinny hanging bridge connecting the two mountains swung in the air, presenting an opportunity for disaster. The bridge could accommodate only one person at a time. They knew the wire would snap.

They dismounted. The fire closed in behind them.

"The box is over there. I'm sure of it," Ciaran said. "Right behind me." Ciaran clasped Madeline's hand and ran across the bridge. Tadgh and Zach followed right behind them. Kyle and Jo came after.

They formed a line and rushed across the swinging bridge.

The fire approached and consumed the horses. The wire snapped, and the bridge dropped from that end, hanging by a thread from the other side. They all clung desperately to the knotted rope of the bridge, knowing it wouldn't hold for long.

From the bottom of the line, Jo began to climb up and over everyone else's bodies. Being petite was certainly an advantage now. She climbed over the edge like a spider. Unravelled a black leather rope wrapped around her waist, she tied it to a stone for purchase and dove down the cliff to grab Ciaran's hand.

"Climb up quick, Kyle," Ciaran said and reached his other hand to grab Madeline's. Madeline reached for Tadgh, and he, in turn, grabbed Zach.

Kyle climbed up quickly from the bottom, then Zach, Tadgh, Madeline, and finally Ciaran.

"Well done, Jo," Ciaran said.

Jo nodded and smiled. Then she moved to stand next to Kyle.

They were in front of the magnificent entrance to a white stone cave. Ciaran and Kyle entered it. The group followed.

In the middle, the cave opened up liked a grand hall. The white stone was illuminated, shedding a mysterious light throughout the cavernous room.

They heard a tapping sound as if an army of people walking on sticks was moving toward them.

A white claw appeared. Then they saw body with many legs.

"Is that a crab? I'm not particularly in the mood for seafood right now," Tadgh said.

"I think it's a white scorpion. It's as big as a cow!" Zach exclaimed incredulously.

"Six of us against a cow-crab. Folks, I think we've got a winner," Madeline joked, shifting her daggers.

Ciaran said to Kyle, "Would you mind taking the left?"

Kyle nodded.

With lightning speed, Ciaran darted to the right, and Kyle moved to the left. They jumped across the tops of a few stones and landed on top of the scorpion. It started to whirl around. Ciaran swung his dagger, and the two eyes of the scorpion flew away. Kyle brought his spear down into the top of the scorpion. A stream of black liquid spilled out and rained down on its white shell.

Suddenly, rows of smaller scorpions appeared from every direction.

"Holy *crab!*" Tadgh said. All of them ran toward the creatures. Daggers swung, spears stabbed. They use whatever weapons they could, stones and sand included, to fight the hard-shelled army.

Chaos.

Ciaran was always right there beside Madeline. Kyle and Jo fought back to back, and Tadgh and Zach did the same.

After a long while, with the cutting off of enough legs, eyes, and claws, the fight came to an end. Some wounded scorpions scurried away. The white shells of hundreds of scorpions littered the ground.

Between them, there were some minor scratches, bruises, and bleeding, but no serious injuries.

"That was easier than I thought." Zach grinned.

"There will be more," Tadgh mumbled as he remembered what he had seen in Ciaran's training.

They walked over the dead scorpions to another compartment of the cave. The light from the white rocks lighted the way.

From a gap between two large rocks, a shadow leaped at Ciaran, pushing him down onto the ground.

CHAPTER 32

An enormous white wolf looked down at Ciaran. He swung his daggers, and the wolf backed off quickly. Suddenly a large pack of them appeared. They stalked the intruders in a circle, looking at the group as if they were their next meal.

Jo swung her rope. It wrapped around the neck of a wolf and ripped its head off in one pull.

Tadgh gasped.

The group broke out into another round of fighting.

After a long while, they had killed several wolves. The wounded ones ran away.

This time they sustained more injuries.

Ciaran helped Madeline up from the ground. "Let me see." He looked at a nasty bite mark on her left wrist. "This will get infected," he mumbled.

Madeline turned him around, inspecting a gash from a claw and a bite mark at the back of his neck. She hadn't covered his back well enough. "This one, too."

Ciaran looked at Tadgh. "Two bites on the legs and one on the left arm. Otherwise, I'm good as new," Tadgh reported.

"A gash on my back and one on my right arm. I can't see my back, but it hurts like hell," Zach said.

"Let me see." Madeline looked. "Oh, it's nasty."

Nearby, Jo was checking her injuries. She was bleeding from both arms and her back. Tadgh approached. Jo gestured for him to keep a distance. He stopped.

Ciaran shrugged off his jacket and tore shreds from it. He secured Madeline's injuries then gave her the remaining part of the jacket. "Could you take care of them, please?" He gestured toward Tadgh and Zach.

"What about you?"

"I'm fine."

Madeline nodded, took the jacket, and went to tend to Tadgh and Zach.

Ciaran stood in the middle of the grand cave and stared at a gigantic illuminated column in the middle. He walked around it. He pressed his hand on the column. It was smooth and icy.

The box has to be here, he thought

Ciaran examined the icy surface. The hundred-foot column held up the ceiling. It was the life support of the grand cave. He noticed a red dot swirling around inside. What was it? Ciaran pulled his dagger out. He anticipated the moving path of the dot and stabbed at it.

The dot stopped moving. A small ice panel in the column slid open, revealing a button. The skin of the column became transparent, and inside, Ciaran could see a box placed at head height.

Everyone approached, looking at it.

"There it is," Kyle said.

He reached his hand out and punched the button.

"Wait!" Ciaran yelled. But it was too late.

The column broke apart. At the same time, the floor cracked and broke away into shards of ice. The column sunk down into the ice water, taking the box with it.

Everyone fled the sinking floor and ran to the rock edges.

The broken floor was now a pond of dark, icy water.

Jo looked at the sinking box. She dove into the water. Ciaran dived in after her. As soon as they disappeared below the surface, the ice sealed over.

Madeline was hanging onto a rock. She had seen this scenario before. She knew exactly what to do. She grabbed as many rocks as she could and slid to the middle of the icy crust to break the surface so that they could escape.

From under the dark water, Ciaran saw the ice closing in. He grabbed Jo to pull her up. She shrugged him off and followed the box down farther. It had slipped away from the broken column and lay at the very bottom. She picked it up. Ciaran grabbed for her again, and they both resurfaced.

Madeline and others had broken the ice and pulled Ciaran and Jo out of the freezing water.

Their bodies were numb. They did not speak.

Madeline held Ciaran. She wrapped her body around him and used whatever she had to give him some warmth. Tadgh darted toward Jo and did the same. He held her in his arms. She grabbed him. Her body shook.

Minutes passed, and Ciaran and Jo finally began to regain some body heat. The color slowly came back into their almost translucent faces. They looked toward each other and then toward the box that was sitting on the floor between them.

Kyle picked up the box. Ciaran slowly brought himself to a standing position. The two men gave each other a measured glance. Tadgh helped Jo to her feet.

Ciaran raised an eyebrow when Kyle gave him the box. He took it. On the lid was a liquid screen and a square panel that said, "Print verification required."

Ciaran smiled. That was why Kyle and Jo had needed him. Jo was a gate-crasher, and Kyle was an exiled Sciphil. Even if they had been able to retrieve the box, they wouldn't have been able to open it.

Ciaran put his palm on the panel to verify. The lid clicked open. Inside the box were two rectangular blocks—one red and one blue. The two blocks were lit up, but Ciaran could not identify what they were made of. A grail was engraved on the red block, and a key was engraved on the blue one.

"The red one is the privilege, and the blue is the invitation," Ciaran said. He turned the box toward Kyle.

Kyle reached out for the red block.

From the corner of Ciaran's eyes, he saw it. Jo raised her arm and slid out her spear while Tadgh watched Ciaran and Kyle.

"Look out, Tadgh!" Ciaran yelled.

It was too late for Tadgh.

Jo pierced her spear right through his heart. She drew it back out.

Tadgh's body slumped to the ground. Ciaran ran toward his brother.

Tadgh was dead.

CHAPTER 33

Jo swung her rope and grabbed the box.

"I want both." That was the first time she had spoken since they had been reunited. What came out was not a voice but the sound of a devil from hell.

She turned and ran with the box.

Ciaran locked his eyes on her back as she fled. He took a stance and threw his dagger.

The dagger hit her right in the back of her head. She slumped down and melted into a pool of black liquid.

"That's not Jo," Ciaran said. He turned around. Kyle had disappeared.

Ciaran dashed toward the box and grabbed it. Then he scrambled back to where Tadgh lay. He crouched next to Tadgh's dead body and opened the box.

He took out the red block—the privilege. On top of the block was another panel. Ciaran pressed his palm against it. A tiny screen appeared on the surface of the block next to the panel. On the screen, the face of a woman appeared. She smiled kindly at him.

"Congratulations. You have gained a privilege. What would you like?"

"My brother has suffered a fatal injury. I want him healed," Ciaran said briskly.

"What is the injury?"

"A stab wound."

"Where?"

"To the heart."

"That is beyond the level of—"

"I don't give a fuck. I gained your privilege. It's supposed to fix anything inside the gate," Ciaran snarled.

"Conditional to—"

"Don't quote terms and conditions to me. I have the invitation as well. I will talk to your Host and will make rest of your life miserable, whoever and wherever you are!"

"But—"

"You offered the privilege. You are required to keep your end of the deal. The Daimon Gate does not break a promise. I want my brother healed. Now!"

"I will consult with my superior." The screen went blank for a long moment. Then a man's face appeared.

"Who is the injured guest?"

"Tadgh LeBlanc."

The man nodded. "He has previously received eudqi from his Sciphil. He is lucky. He will be fine. Step aside please."

Ciaran stepped aside.

A curtain of light poured down around Tadgh. They could not see him anymore.

Ciaran turned around. Madeline knew he was looking for her. She pulled him into her arms. Ciaran clung to her. He held on tight. He buried his head against her shoulder, and she felt the heat of his tears.

Madeline said nothing. She just embraced him.

After a long while, the light curtain vanished. Tadgh lay motionless on the floor and then opened his eyes. He looked around to gain his bearings.

Ciaran scrambled toward him. "How are you feeling?" he asked.

Tadgh winced and looked down at his chest. His shirt was still open, revealing a rapidly healing wound. Ciaran helped him up.

"Let's get you out of here," Ciaran said.

At the entrance of the cave, Ciaran sat Tadgh down on a rock. He pointed to the top of the hill, where the light reflection looked like a rainbow.

"That's the exit out of the Daimon Gate," Ciaran said.

"Kyle!"

In the distance, they could see Kyle charging toward the exit. He was carrying a large box nearly the size of a coffin on his shoulder as if it was a toy.

"I'll cut him into pieces," Ciaran growled.

Kyle seemed to be annoyed and threw the box to the ground. He pulled Jo out of it.

"That's the real Jo. I can read her. I can see her mind," Madeline gasped.

Tadgh frowned. "It's her. She's scared and angry," he whispered and quickly ran out of breath just by voicing that short sentence. He could see Jo's emotions now, but he couldn't go and get her.

Ciaran watched Kyle dragging Jo toward the exit. He could send in a blade and cut Kyle into pieces right now. He wanted to kill him so badly.

Jo kicked, screamed, and wriggled out of Kyle's grip. She turned around and pulled out the knife she'd hidden in her secret pocket, the one she had stolen from the zombie gangster on Earth. She stabbed Kyle. The small knife didn't do much damage, but it distracted him and stopped him from dragging her further toward the exit.

Ciaran clenched his fists. He could feel his fury coming to the surface. If he sent in the blade, it would kill both Kyle and Jo. If he let Kyle go, there would be consequences when he fled to the other universes.

Tadgh was too weak to make a run for Jo. Ciaran knew Tadgh wouldn't ask him to hold back on this important decision, but he knew how important Jo was to his brother.

The devastation in Tadgh's eyes cut at him. He had almost lost his brother. He couldn't give Tadgh another hit by killing Jo right in front of him.

Ciaran withheld the blade.

Jo ran down the hill.

Kyle fled through the exit.

Jo hurried toward Tadgh. She grabbed him and stared at the wound on his chest. "You're hurt. Oh, my God. Did Kyle do this to you?" Tears rolled down her face. "I'm sorry I wasn't there for you."

"I'm okay. Everything is fine now." He wiped the tears from her face and pulled her into his arms.

"I know it's useless to ask you to leave the gate before I do. But I have one thing to see to before we leave. Could you wait for me here?" Ciaran said.

"You're going back in for Bran, aren't you?" Madeline asked.

Ciaran nodded. "It shouldn't take long. And it's neither hard nor dangerous. During his last trip, Bran became lost and has been trapped in the oblivion for a long time. This invitation will help me navigate to him, and I'll get him out. I promised him this. Okay? There won't be any fighting or struggles."

"Is that all?" Madeline asked.

"That's all. I'll get him out, and he'll tell me where Mother is. That's the deal. That's it."

Tadgh tried to say something. Ciaran bent down. He shook Tadgh's shoulders gently and looked into his brother's eyes, the feature with the strongest resemblance between them.

"I can't handle another episode from you, Tadgh. Please stay here. Leave with them if you must."

Tadgh nodded and closed his eyes, leaning against the rock to rest.

CHAPTER 34

Ciaran went back into the cave. He pulled out the blue block. It lit up in the dark. He walked slowly. The light would be strongest when heading in the right direction. That was what Bran had told him. He went deeper and deeper into the cave.

The stone had gone from white to black. The temperature increased. The sound of water dripping somewhere between the rocks sang like music.

Ciaran entered a wide grand hall where he found a black rock arch. He touched the rocks. A wave of strange current pulsed out like electricity. Ciaran reached his hand out into the empty space on the other side of the arched rocks.

His hand disappeared in front of him. He withdrew his hand.

The dimensional gate to the oblivion, he thought. That was where Bran was.

Ciaran pushed the blue block through the gateway to the other side, and unlike his hand which seemed to vanish, he could still see the illuminated block.

Ciaran nodded to himself and was happy with the compass he had in his hand. He walked through the archway.

He was immediately transferred to a peaceful green meadow. He shrugged. Oblivion didn't look bad at all. In the distance, a small cottage blended nicely into the setting. It was like a live painting of the countryside in England, Ciaran thought.

In front of the cottage, Bran stood like a farmer, a shovel in one hand and a bucket in the other.

Ciaran approached. "Bran."

"Ciaran. I knew you would make it. Having you as a successor was the best decision I ever made."

"It's my honor. We should leave now. People are waiting."

Bran nodded. "Let me get out of this farmer gear and get my stuff. Come on in."

They entered the door of the so-called cottage. The door was so small that Ciaran had to bend down to squeeze through.

Inside the tiny cottage was a gigantic space station. Ciaran turned around. He could still see the meadow through the door. *How is this even possible?* he thought.

Ciaran pointed toward the door. "Is that a dimensional gate?"

Bran laughed. "You certainly don't disappoint. It is, indeed." Bran gestured widely. "And this is *my* dimension. I created it."

"You created a dimension? How?"

"You have a lot to learn, Ciaran. But now you should have some confidence in the impact of what I asked you to do. You should know how significant your role will be in the history of the multiverse. And you should appreciate what I have given you from Eudaiz."

Bran entered a series of commands into computer units that were as large as the wall of the space station. He pointed to the flashing light on a control panel.

Ciaran approached. The monitor asked for print verification. He pressed his palm to the square panel. A burning sensation ran up his arm and his spine and shocked his brain.

Ciaran grunted and passed out on the floor.

When he came to, Bran was working on a computer.

"You're very strong Ciaran. We are good to go now."

Ciaran stood up, looking at his hand. There was no mark on his palm. He didn't feel any different.

"What did you do to me?"

"Nothing really. I just helped you out with your task. The information I asked you to collect would be a lot to remember using an ordinary human brain. I simply added more memory capacity to yours. That's all."

"How long have I been out?"

"Just a few seconds."

He pushed up from his chair and led the way out of the cottage.

"You're not taking anything? Your equipment?"

"No, I loaded everything into you. I trust you." Bran patted Ciaran's shoulder.

Moments later, they were using the blue block to navigate their way back to the black stone arch. Ciaran pointed to it. "That's a dimensional gate. That's why you got lost."

"I wasn't lost."

"What?"

"I knew it was a dimensional gate. Kyle stabbed me through it. He snatched Madeline from her cot and ran through the Daimon Gate. I chased him to get the baby back. We fought. I wounded him badly, but when he pushed the baby in front of me, I hesitated. That's how he got me. Then the dimension shifted. Without a navigator, I couldn't get back out."

Ciaran nodded. "Well, you got yourself a good Sciphil One now, thanks to Kyle."

They walked through the gate and returned to the entrance of the cave.

Madeline rushed toward Ciaran. Everything in her body and mind told her that things were not going well.

"Darling, are you okay?" Ciaran asked.

"We need to leave. We should leave right now, Ciaran."

"Yes, of course." He held Madeline and felt her body shaking.

"Why don't you sit down for a moment?" Ciaran said.

"No, no. We have to leave. Right now."

"She's been like this for ten minutes. We can leave now, Madeline," Jo said. She turned around to help Tadgh, who was still weak and dazed.

"Ciaran needs to say goodbye to the Host before we leave, Madeline. It would be very inappropriate if he didn't do so," Bran said.

"What? No, no. We are leaving right now!" Madeline insisted.

"Madeline, I just need to say goodbye. I have the invitation. It will only take five minutes. Then we'll leave. You'll have Bran here with you. If Kyle comes back—"

"No, no, not Kyle. It's not Kyle. It's something else. Something is really wrong. Please don't go in again," Madeline cried.

"Bran." Ciaran looked at Bran.

"You have to, Ciaran. Don't you want to find out about your mother?"

"She—" Ciaran looked at Madeline.

"You've just been through the Daimon Gate. It's a lot to take in. I'd be surprised if she weren't emotional. Let's finish this quickly. I want to leave, too," Bran said.

"If anything—"

"Nothing will happen to you. But yes, I will take care of everyone. I have the power to keep the promise. I am the current king of Eudaiz, remember?" Bran said.

Ciaran hesitated.

"Look, Jo can't exit the gate without getting killed because she didn't have an invitation to enter. As the current king of Eudaiz, I can give her the invitation now." Bran grabbed Jo's hand and pressed his thumbprint to it. "This is a temporary entry for guests. She will be fine. I keep my promises. I hope you keep yours, Ciaran."

Madeline wrapped her arms around Ciaran. She knew she could not make him stay.

Her body ached. Her heart ached. She could not explain her feelings to him. She could not find a reason for him to stay. She reached up and kissed him as if it would be their last kiss.

She looked at Ciaran going back into the cave. Her knees buckled, and Zach caught her. He carried her to the edge of the rock where she was violently ill.

CHAPTER 35

Ciaran walked along the white stone hall to an entrance. He followed the signal on the blue block. A panel slid open. He inserted the block, and a wall-sized door opened widely, revealing a grand reception room.

Ciaran had butterflies in his stomach.

The room arrangement and decoration closely resembled that of Mon Ciel. An automatic voice echoed across the room, "Welcome Ciaran Leblanc. The Host invites you to take a tour of the EYE before meeting in the Great Reception."

Even the name of the room was the same as Mon Ciel. He wouldn't be surprised to find his mother here. But he let go of that speculation for the moment and focused on the task at hand.

All he had to do was to go to the EYE, the most sophisticated computer system in the cosmos, and download the data for Bran. Once he completed that task, anything else would be a bonus. If he met his mother here, great. If not, Bran would tell him where she was.

A steel door in front of him slid open. Ciaran entered an eye-shaped room. The walls were covered with monitors, each flashing with images. It was like an enormous cinema that showed thousands of movies at the same time.

The control panel flashed for print verification. Ciaran pressed his palm on the panel, and text appeared.

Ciaran LeBlanc.
One invitation: Available.
One privilege: Claimed.
Data access: FULL.

Ciaran nodded. As Bran had predicted, he had full access to the data. He walked around the room and glanced at the panels. He recognized the faces of the prince and the princess at the Red Castle. He touched the screen. Text appeared.

Factual:
Prince and Princess of the Red Castle.
Status: Sentenced to death by a thousand lightning bolts.
Execution date: Five thousand five hundred – twenty two – sixteen – sixth quarter.
Crime: Manipulating the Daimon Gate system for personal gain.
Preview: Y/N
Ciaran typed: *Y*

The prince and the princess had not yet been executed. There was still hope, Ciaran mused. He made a mental note of the execution date. He had to ask Tadgh to translate the date into something more sensible.

A stream of images flooded the screen. Ciaran washing onto the shore. The princess finding him, taking him home, and tending to his injuries. Being fed the inducer. Ciaran and Madeline in a subconscious state. The two of them sharing their vows and consummating their marriage. Leaving the Red Castle.

It was exactly as the prince had said. The system captured everything—the conscious and subconscious levels of every living thing inside the gate. Ciaran promised himself he would come back and rectify this death sentence now that he knew how.

The screen flashed: *Download data: Y/N*
Ciaran typed: *N*.
Then he typed in: *Search Bran LeBlanc.*

The computer flashed:
Factual:
Bran LeBlanc - Sciphil Three - King of Eudaiz.
Qualification: Pass Daimon Gate.
Black stage: Ten challenges, gatekeeper: Simon Bannon.
White stage: Five challenges, gatekeeper: Lucas Masr.
Red stage: Twenty challenges, consummated with Jennifer Wyse, gatekeeper: Martin Chinxz.
Preview: Y/N

Jennifer Wyse was his mother's maiden name. Ciaran typed: *N* to decline the preview. Then he searched for Jennifer Wyse.

The computer flashed:
Factual:

Jennifer Wyse, now Jennifer LeBlanc - Hostess of the Daimon Gate.

Family status: Married to Conan LeBlanc, children: Ciaran LeBlanc and Tadgh LeBlanc.

Past marriage: Bran LeBlanc.

Past position: Sciphil Six.

Qualification: Pass Daimon Gate.

Black stage: Ten challenges, gatekeeper: Simon Bannon.

White stage: Five challenges, gatekeeper: Lucas Masr.

Red stage: Twenty challenges, consummated with Bran LeBlanc, gatekeeper: Martin Chinxz.

Preview: Y/N

His mother had gone through the gate at the same time, and she had married Bran. They must have divorced afterward, and then she resigned from her Sciphil Six position. That was plausible. If she was now the Hostess of Daimon Gate, Ciaran would see her soon. Ciaran typed: N to decline the preview. Then he searched for Madeline Kelley.

The computer flashed:

Factual:

Madeline Kelley, now Madeline LeBlanc.

Family status: Married to Ciaran LeBlanc, children: Son and daughter, not yet named.

Current position: Sciphil One - appointment in progress.

Qualification: Pass Daimon Gate.

Black stage: Five challenges, gatekeeper: Snitxc Mitchell.

White stage: Six challenges, gatekeeper: Laureen White.

Red stage: Zero challenges, consummated with Ciaran LeBlanc, gatekeepers: Lecal Brandon and Leciel Brandon.

Preview: Y/N

Ciaran could not withhold a smile—he was to have a son and a daughter with Madeline! Their consummation had conceived their children. They had twins. He was a father! How was this even possible? He didn't know. He didn't care. He was just happy.

The EYE was genius—it recorded everything, Ciaran thought. He could not resist a preview of this.

On the screen, Ciaran saw them making love at the Red Castle. Under the light of the eternal flame, she was beautiful. That moment was the most sensational experience he had ever experienced.

They had made love before. Several times. But at the Red Castle, the experience was profound.

It was a rebirth of their love and lives together as soul mates.

On the screen, a line of text appeared: Transmutation rebirth. Children conceived.

Ciaran shook his head, astonished. The EYE must record information down to the level of the atom.

The screen flashed: *Download data: Y/N.*

Ciaran typed: *N.*

He glanced at the other screens. Billions of images flew by. The lives and events of everyone and everything that had ever occurred in the multiverse.

Ciaran recognized events on Earth. Some were as significant as world wars, and some were as minor as a spat between neighbors about whose dog had shit in whose yard. Ciaran was sure the EYE had recorded which dog had committed the crime. He wondered whether the people engaged in the argument over the dog's business would ever be informed of the data.

On a bigger scale, the EYE must have recorded factual information behind all of the scandals and mysteries on Earth. If that were discovered, Ciaran was sure that it would change the history of humankind.

He looked at his left palm. All he had to do was to download the data for Bran by pressing his palm against the control panel. Would the capacity of the memory Bran had designed be large enough for this database? Ciaran didn't think so.

He wagered Bran only wanted to establish the connection. Having access to this kind of information was equivalent to having the power of the creator of all things. Knowing everything that anyone had ever done in any world.

This was the power of God.

The computer continued to flash: *Viewing will end in ten seconds. Download Data Y/N?*

Ciaran pressed *N* again.

The room lit up. A door to the next room slid open. Ciaran walked into a reception room which was almost identical to the one at Mon Ciel.

CHAPTER 36

At the end of the long table sat a man Ciaran was not surprised to see—his father, Conan LeBlanc.

Ciaran approached slowly, calm and sure.

Conan gestured toward a chair.

Ciaran sat and gazed at his father.

"Congratulations for passing the Daimon Gate," Conan said.

"Thank you," Ciaran said dryly.

"Children conceived during the Red stage of the transmutation process are the best human beings. You should reward yourself and Madeline for that."

"I believe in nurture, not nature. Our children will grow up within our care and protection. They will turn out the way they want to be, not the way we want them to be. And they do not have to be the best just because they were conceived in a spiritual space."

"A man in your position has to bring his children up the right way—"

"Did you?" Ciaran cut him off. "For twenty years you let me believe you were dead. You left Tadgh and me scrambling to live up to your expectations. You let Mother struggle on her own with a brat like me when she'd have been better off to smother me as a baby."

Ciaran hurled the entire tea set that sat on the table before him at the wall.

"You still don't handle your rage well, Ciaran."

"The fuck I don't."

"I've been watching over you and Tadgh."

"Right, stalking us using your EYE system. Did you see how many times Tadgh almost died in the last few weeks? Did you see how many times we were attacked when we were off guard? And you just watched for entertainment?"

"I cannot interfere. I can only observe. There are rules."

"A man in your position has to do the right thing, don't you? You would do the right thing by your world, whatever it is, but not by your family, the world you created and abandoned in the blink of an eye."

Ciaran shook his head. He wanted to laugh at the coincidence of the expression the blink of an eye, but he speculated it wouldn't erupt as a laugh but a roar of anger. The rage threatened to consume him, but he squelched it.

"Tell me if Mother is okay, and I'll get out of your hair."

"She is the Hostess here. She is quite well."

Ciaran pushed up.

"Very well then. Goodbye, Father." He walked toward the door.

"Do you think this is a familial matter?"

"What else could it be?"

"You passed the worthiness test. You could be the next Host of the Daimon Gate if you are interested."

Ciaran cast a cold look at Conan. "Another fucking test? No, I don't care, and I'm not interested." He turned around again to leave.

"You're not going to leave just like that, are you?"

"Trust me, you'll want me to leave before I do a lot of damage to this place."

"More than that broken tea set?"

Ciaran gave his father a blank stare. "If you have anything else to say to complete this formality, please do it quickly, Host of the Daimon Gate."

"Don't you even want to see your mother?"

"You said she's well. That's good enough."

"So you trust me?"

"No. But Mother stuck by you for that long, so I figure she must love you. If she's happy, that's good enough for me."

Conan nodded. "You're a greater man that you give yourself credit for, Ciaran. You've seen the power of the EYE, you had full access, and yet you did not download the data."

"I don't have a use for the data. And I hope a man in your position would do the right thing, too."

Conan nodded. "You don't need the data for personal use. But if you are the King-to-be of Eudaiz, it will prove to be very beneficial to you. Why didn't you take it?"

"That's my decision and none of your business."

"If someone wants to steal the data from the EYE, that is my business. Anything that happens inside this gate is my business."

"I didn't take the data. What else do you want me to say?"

"Conspiracy to steal is the same crime as actually stealing it. Within this gate, the penalty is death by a thousand lightning bolts."

"I don't see how this is relevant. I'm not taking anything. Consider this conversation finished."

"If I asked you to press your left palm against a detective panel, would I find anything?"

Silence.

"Why are you protecting him, Ciaran?"

"I'll talk him out of this."

Conan laughed. "You're too confident, Ciaran. Bran has been plotting this for more than thirty years, and you think you can talk him out of it?"

"If you knew, why didn't you stop him?"

"The oblivion is a black hole. We don't have access although it is a part of the gate and within my jurisdiction. We've been waiting for him to come out for a long time. Now he's back inside the gate. I will take him before he exits."

"I'm not helping you to get Bran."

"You don't have to do anything. Just stay here. I'll send someone to get him. When we detect the device is from him, that's will be the end of him."

Ciaran shook his head and said nothing. He shifted his sore shoulder. "What if you don't find anything on Bran?"

Conan was in the process of calling his people. He stopped. "Then I'll have to let him go. But an operation like this is quite major. He is the current King of Eudaiz. Our council will question my conduct, and I will have to resign. I know he's guilty. But if it is God's will that he passes this time, then so be it."

"What do you mean by *this* time?"

The door to the room flung wide open.

Jennifer sauntered in, more beautiful than ever. She wore a long white robe, and her face was radiant. Her eyes warmed at the sight of Ciaran.

Ciaran stood up. "You look well, Mother."

"And you look terrible, Son. I know that passing the Daimon Gate for the first time is very taxing. But it shouldn't have put you in such poor condition. Is that why you locked me up? So I would miss his visit, Conan?"

"I don't know what you're talking about," Conan said.

"Oh, well, maybe it was just a bad luck then. I see that Bran is waiting at the exit. Would you let him go, darling? Ciaran, stay for tea with me, will you?"

"Mother."

Conan continued to call people. He puzzled at the panel.

"I sent them on some tasks, and they're busy right now. Do you need the troop for anything in particular? There is no fight simulation on at the moment," Jennifer said.

Conan cleared his throat. "No, that's fine." He glanced at Ciaran.

"I sent my secretary to the exit to tell Bran and his people not to wait as Ciaran will stay for tea."

"Jennifer," Conan lowered his voice.

"They should have gotten the message by now . . ."

Conan rushed toward the monitor, and Jennifer grabbed him.

"It's too late. Conan. Let Bran go."

Conan grabbed Jennifer's shoulders as if he were about to shake her. Ciaran snatched Conan and threw him against a wall. Ciaran stood in front of his mother.

Conan straightened up and let out a discerning chuckle. "Right. Mother and son team up. Like I don't know what I'm doing here? I'm useless. I'm just so useless."

"Why can't you let it go, Conan?" Jennifer asked. "Everything will be fine."

She approached Conan. Tears rolled down her face. It was the first time Ciaran had seen his mother cry. Conan wiped the tears from her face.

"I'll resign. We'll leave here," Conan said.

Jennifer nodded. Conan held his wife tightly in his arms.

"Let's leave. Forget about all this," he whispered.

"Can you at least tell me what's going on here?" Ciaran asked.

The monitor made a verbal announcement. "Bran LeBlanc requesting a call."

Conan pointed at the monitor. "You see, he's the one who's not letting go. I'll have to call this in. I have to catch him."

"What did he do?" Ciaran asked.

"Don't tell him, Conan. It won't help."

"He tested weapons on small stars in remote galaxies and killed billions of residents. Do you expect me to see billions of people killed and ignore it just because it was outside of my jurisdiction?" Conan snarled.

"It's not just outside of your jurisdiction. There's a death penalty for interfering with any affairs outside the gate. You don't even have soldiers. Bran is a powerful man. You have nothing but your good intentions, and those won't be able to to save you."

"How can I be a righteous man, a virtuous gatekeeper, if I ignore this opportunity to do the right thing by billions of innocents? Is that the sort of man you want to be with, Jennifer?"

Jennifer cried out. "I don't want a saint. I am only a wife. I need a husband, and our children need a father."

"Child. Not children, Jennifer."

Conan punched the wall after these words slipped out of his mouth.

CHAPTER 37

After punching the wall, Conan turned back and approached Jennifer. She backed away.

"Don't come near me," she said.

Ciaran pulled her into his arms. "I'm sorry, Mother."

He looked at Conan. A searing pain raised in his heart. Whatever had happened between them, he still saw Conan as his father.

Ciaran remembered the data reported his mother's ex-marriage to Bran. That meant he was Bran's son. He looked at Conan. "I'm not yours then? I assume your jealousy plays a role in this attempt to arrest Bran?" Ciaran spoke to Conan.

Conan slumped into a chair and said nothing.

It was strange. His mother pulled him into her arms and held on as if she wanted to savor the moment for as long as she could. She kissed his cheek and his forehead. Then she released him. *What was she trying to do?* Ciaran thought.

"Regardless of how bad of a man Bran is, you love him because he is your little brother, Conan," Jennifer said.

Conan nodded and put his head in his hands. "I'm sorry, darling."

"Don't be," she continued. "The only way to end Bran is to illegitimize his qualification for the Daimon Gate or expose his attempt to steal the data from the EYE. The second solution is dangerous because if you can't expose him, your head will be on the chopping block. On those grounds, I will not let either of you go near Bran."

"If he walks out the gate this time, all those people he killed will never have justice. I'll not have another chance at this. We have to get him now, inside the gate," Conan said.

"You are not getting him with the data. I won't risk you or Ciaran doing that."

"I'm not a crystal vase, Mother."

Jennifer glanced at Ciaran. He turned on his heels and sat down at the table.

"I'll get him with the qualification. He cheated at the Red stage. If I can provide evidence of that, he will be disqualified from his kingship. While he's still inside the gate, the penalty for manipulating the system for personal gain is death by a thousand lightning bolts. With his kingship disqualified, he will be ended at the source in Eudaiz, too. If you both want him to go down that way, I'm happy to assist," Jennifer said dryly.

Both Ciaran and Conan gave Jennifer blank stares.

"What evidence?" Ciaran asked.

"The EYE's data cannot be manipulated," Conan said.

"You underestimate your brother. Your training to be the Daimon Gate Host was a secret to the multiverse, but not to Bran. He knew I wanted to pay you a visit and I missed you, but I couldn't tell anyone. Bran told me he could lobby for me to go through the gate as Sciphil Six's successor. It was just a play. Then I could go in and out of the gate to visit you. I was stupid enough to believe him."

Conan stood up. Jennifer gestured him not to approach her.

"Bran was going through the qualifying process as the King-to-be of Eudaiz. He trained me so that I could go through the gate with him. We went through the gate and passed all the stages, and at the Red stage, he forced me to consummate."

"What do you mean by him forcing you?" Ciaran's voice was dangerously low. The pain pounded in his head. The heat of the Red stage still lingered in him. It was hell.

And he wouldn't have passed if Madeline hadn't gone down to look for him. He would have been forced to take another queen. Which he wouldn't have done. And then he would have been killed.

Bran knew all this. He wanted to ensure he had the queen with him. Someone he could trust, and someone who foolishly trusted him.

There was no response from his mother, so he asked again, "What do you mean by him forcing you?"

"I mean that I didn't consent to be his wife. But he manipulated the data and blackmailed the gatekeeper to cheat the system. Martin Chinxz was the gatekeeper. He took pity on me. He gave me a copy of the original data. He died a few years later of 'natural causes'—you were naive enough to believe that, Conan!"

"If you show the council the original record, you will be charged with withholding it," Conan said.

"Then I'd plead guilty. I was a victim. The penalty shouldn't be too severe. Martin Chinxz died.

I can claim fear, shame, or whatever reason you can think of . . ."

While his mother ranted about the plan to convict Bran, Ciaran broke into her portable databank.

He had activated and played the record of her original. She had passcodes and locks on the file, but opening these portable databank locks was child's play for Ciaran.

As soon as the data came on the screen, his blood ran cold. "Is this the original record?" he asked and turned the monitor around so that his mother and Conan could see it.

He could see in his mother's eyes that, although she had not watched it for years, the incident was still raw in her memory.

On the monitor was the scene of her being raped and beaten.

Compared to the hell that he went through at the Red stage and the condition of the creatures in the form of women who had been ripped of all dignity, his mother's condition was far worse.

As the female companion, a contender to be queen, Madeline was well protected by his love and her love for him. They were unified. That was how they got through.

His mother had gotten nothing. She didn't love Bran, didn't agree to marry him, and thus shouldn't have even been in the Red stage. Bran had only wanted a queen, and he didn't love her. They weren't soul mates. He couldn't and wouldn't have protected her.

He had merely wanted a queen to consummate so that he could pass the gate and became king.

His mother had been on her own, against everything and everyone in the gate.

The pain in his head was unbearable. He was afraid his fury would surface. But if it did, who would it kill?

In the corner of the screen was the text: *Transmutation rebirth. Child conceived.*

Ciaran shook his head. That child was him.

That was how he had been born. The best human being conceived in the Red stage of the transmutation process. Even the spiritual system disregarded human emotions. He had been conceived at the best astronomical moment and had inherited the best from his parents.

What could his mother have done apart from swallowing the truth and raising her child? If Bran could replace the data, what would be his mother's chances of proving that her record was the original? Between the words of the King of Eudaiz and a young girl, foolishly in love, who had agreed to pass all other stages of the Daimon Gate test with her man, who would the authorities believe?

Jennifer charged at Ciaran. She slapped him in the face. "How dare you!"

Ciaran pulled his mother into his arms and let her cry.

He saw stars in his eyes. Black stars of fury. They needed to consume. They needed to kill. He needed to destroy.

Tears rolled down Conan's face. He knew his wife had been forced. But he obviously hadn't realized the extent of it. And he had not known about the record. Somewhere in the back of his mind, he did not believe her at times.

The record of the EYE was flawless. It was the best computer system in the cosmos. It was the system he had sworn to protect.

After a moment, Ciaran asked, "Does Bran know about me?"

Jennifer shook her head. "He didn't look at the original—he was in too much of a hurry to replace it."

The computer announced Bran's request again.

Conan punched at the control button. "Tell him just a few minutes."

Ciaran picked his mother up, walked her to the room next door, and gently placed her down on a reading chair. He walked out, closed the door, jammed it from the outside, and ignored her cries to be released.

"I'm going to get Bran inside the gate for you. Do you trust me?" Ciaran asked Conan.

"But—"

"Do you want Mother to report that tape?"

"No, but—"

"I'll need some data from the EYE. Just a little."

"I can't let you download any data."

"If I can get Bran inside the gate, then everything should be fine, am I correct?"

Conan nodded.

"Then let's do it."

Before leaving, Ciaran said, "Again, I believe in nurture. I only have—and accept—one father."

Conan nodded. "And I have two sons, both of whom I love more than anything."

"Let's keep it that way."

CHAPTER 38

A moment later, Ciaran walked toward the exit, where Bran was waiting. He saw that Madeline, Zach, and Tadgh had been moved into the transitional zone. They could see into but could not re-enter the gate.

Tears streamed down Madeline's face. She had an incredible sixth sense. She must know disaster was coming. Madeline, his wife, his children's mother—she was beautiful. Ciaran wanted to rush to her and kiss her, but he knew it was best not to make Bran suspect.

"What took so long?" Bran asked.

"Didn't you get the message? My mother was in there. She wanted me to stay for tea!"

Bran nodded. "As I suspected, she's the Hostess, isn't she?"

Ciaran nodded. "Can we go now?"

"I have to make sure that you got the data first. Once we are out of here, there will be no chance for us to get back to the EYE."

"I got the data. How do you want to check it?"

Bran contemplated. "Let's connect when we get to Eudaiz." He turned around to leave.

"Sure." Ciaran followed, walking as slowly as he could.

"What's the matter?"

"Nothing. Just a little pain."

"I'll see to it when we settle."

"Why did you want the data on rural planning and plantations?"

Bran stopped. "What?"

Ciaran shrugged. "I saw part of the data before downloading."

Bran narrowed his eyes, "Are you sure you got the right data?"

"If I recall correctly, you wanted the data in the EYE system, right?"

"That's correct."

"That's it then. Time was limited. I could only download some of the categories, whichever came first."

"What? Was the access granted to all categories?"

"I'm not sure. Let's go," Ciaran said and strode toward the exit.

"No, no, if we go, we can't get back in."

"I'm not going back in. Why don't you do it yourself?"

Bran looked directly into Ciaran's eyes. "You're not trying to trick me, are you, Ciaran?"

"What reason would I have to do that?"

"I can still withdraw your successor role. If I do it now before you exit the gate, you will be a gate-crasher. That will be a sentence of death by a thousand lightning bolts."

"Remember, Bran, I promised to do this for you in exchange for information about my mother. Now I know that my mother is well and good. Why would I want to do anything to you?"

Bran nodded. "I'm sorry. Okay. Let's just check the data before we go."

"I want to get to my wife. So whatever you want to do in here, do it quickly."

"Give me your left hand."

Bran reached his right hand out and clasped Ciaran's left palm as if they were engaged in a handshake.

As soon as their hands connected, Ciaran could feel a current run from his spine to his palm. Bran's eyes went blank as if he was looking into the distance. Then he snapped back quickly and tried to withdraw his hand.

Ciaran clasped Bran's hand tighter and would not let go.

"What's wrong?" Ciaran asked.

Bran's eyes darkened. "You son of a bitch." Bran pulled his hand hard, trying to yank it out of Ciaran's grip.

Ciaran predicted that Bran had now left his digital imprint at the EYE databank—proof of his attempt to gain access. Ciaran looked up and saw sparks of oncoming lightning bolts. He let Bran's hand go.

"This is for what you did to my mother. You don't deserve her."

"I won't go down alone, Ciaran." Bran looked up and saw the lightning coming his way.

Out of the corner of his eye, Ciaran saw Conan and his mother desperately running toward him. They gestured for him to get out.

Ciaran withdrew out of the exit.

Bran saw the opportunity and ran back toward the black arched stone to go back to the oblivion. They could not get him from the black hole.

Ciaran tackled him and pushed him back to the exit zone.

From the transitional zone, Madeline, Tadgh, and Zach tried to re-enter without success. They witnessed Bran and Ciaran struggling for reasons unknown to them.

Bran drew his King Sciphil sword. "I'm not going down alone, Ciaran. You'll have to share these thousand lightning bolts with me."

He charged at Ciaran with the sword. Ciaran pulled out his daggers. They fought.

Although Bran was an old man, he was King Sciphil. At this stage, Ciaran was only a human. Bran kicked Ciaran to the ground.

"Ciaran LeBlanc, I renounce your role as my successor."

Bran tried to grab Ciaran's left arm where he had the golden crucifix. Ciaran withdrew.

"I do not accept."

He rolled away and kicked Bran back into the exit zone.

Madeline, Tadgh, and Zach were being transported further away and were near the end of the transitional zone. Ciaran glanced quickly at the tears on Madeline's face.

Bran charged out of the exit zone again. Ciaran had to force him back in with a weapon fight.

The daggers and sword clashed and ignited sparks. Ciaran locked the sword against a stone with his two daggers. Bran pulled at the sword but could not move it from the stone. Ciaran snatched Bran and spun him around. Bran fell to the ground.

Ciaran used his body weight to pin him down to the ground. He was about to land a punch on Bran's face.

But he couldn't do it. He could kill Bran with a weapon—and he would. But he could not find the will to use his fist on the man who had created him.

Bran looked up at Ciaran from the ground. For a brief moment, Bran registered something so profound that he could not explain it—a blood connection between them.

Bran shoved Ciaran away and stood up.

They eyed each other, saying nothing.

The lightning bolts drew nearer.

Conan and Jennifer approached from the other direction.

Thunder rumbled in from outside the gate.

Madeline, Tadgh, and Zach were outside the gate, and it started to close.

Madeline saw the lightning storm right above where Ciaran and Bran were standing.

She screamed, but she knew Ciaran couldn't hear her.

A bolt of lightning knocked Ciaran off his feet and threw him out of the exit zone.

Others started striking Bran. He blocked one. He blocked another. And then he was hit. He slumped to the ground. He stood up quickly, roared, and ran toward the closing gate. More lightning bolts fenced him in. He could run no longer. He stood and took the hits.

He looked at Ciaran. Ciaran couldn't hear him, but he was sure Bran said, "I forgive you."

Ciaran stood up.

His mother and Conan continued to run toward the zone. Lightning bolts struck everywhere in hundreds of blazing colors. It was difficult to see Bran now, but through a little gap in the bolts, Ciaran caught a glimpse of him.

Madeline stood numbly, gazing through the remaining slit in the closing gate at what was happening.

There was a whirl of light as the burning King Sciphil sword flew out from the forest of lightning bolts toward Jennifer. Conan darted forward, pushing Jennifer aside. All he could do was watch it flying directly toward him.

Conan knew it would be the end. He would take the sword from his brother.

A body flew in front of Conan, blocking the sword's path.

Ciaran dropped to the ground. The sword had pierced his body.

Ciaran reeled up. He pulled the sword out and threw it toward the forest of lightning bolts.

The sword pinned Bran's body to the stone, where he stood immobile and died.

Blood streamed out of the wound in Ciaran's body. He fell to the ground.

That was the last thing Madeline saw.

The gate closed.

Darkness.

CHAPTER 39

Madeline woke in Ayana's arms. She had passed out for a brief moment when she saw the last image of Ciaran before the Daimon Gate closed.

She could accept that he might die. But she could not accept the gate between them. He might die, but they could not be in two different worlds when it happened.

Madeline shrugged off Ayana's supporting arms.

"Take me back inside the gate, please."

Taking one look at Madeline, Ayana understood that nothing she said or did now could waver her determination. She nodded.

Ayana reopened the gate.

Madeline charged inside, followed by Tadgh, Zach, Jo, Ayana, and Pete.

***

The air in the exit zone was thick with smoke and the acrid smell of something burning. The scorched ground encircled a large area. Bran's dead body was still pinned to the stone.

In the corner, Jennifer was holding Ciaran's body in her arms.

"Oh, God." Tadgh's face expressed pure anguish. Conan approached, pulling Tadgh into his arms and letting him cry.

Zach saw no tears on Madeline's face. She was as cold as steel.

Madeline crouched next to Jennifer.

"Could I take a look at him, please?"

"He's dead. I killed my son."

"Please," she repeated.

Jennifer looked at Madeline and released Ciaran.

Madeline needed no medical knowledge to know that Ciaran was gone. But her sixth sense told her to believe otherwise. That was all she had at the moment. Her sixth sense guided by her Daimon.

She would do whatever it took to protect the happiness she had fought for and serve.

Madeline looked at Bran's body, and she puzzled.

She reached down and kissed Ciaran's still-warm face. Then she flew across the scorched ground toward Bran. Madeline pulled at the King Sciphil sword that pinned him to the stone. Bran's body instantly disintegrated into the air, the same way Juliette's body had exploded under the two thousand light beams.

Before anyone could react or say anything, the ground rumbled and shook.

The sound of an explosion came through the gate and shook the ground again.

"A reformation," Ayana mumbled.

The gate spun open. Bran re-entered the gate at great speed in spectacular form—a form that resembled that of his glorious days. Tears streamed down Ayana's face when she caught sight of him.

Conan ran in front of everyone, blocking Bran. The two brothers snarled at each other and whirled around like two male lions guarding their territories and testing their prowess.

"Have you ever seen a King of Eudaiz die inside the gate, Conan?"

"I underestimated you . . ."

"You did that all your life, brother. That sword was for you, not for him."

"He took it. I couldn't stop him."

Bran raised his hand, and his sword returned to him instantly. He pointed it at Conan. "If I do it again, will you take the sword this time?"

Jennifer stood in front of Conan. "Please don't kill him, Bran."

"Yes, I'll take your sword. If I can take it and wash away your sins, I will," Conan said.

Bran pushed the sword forward, pressing it to Conan's throat. "You'd stand there and take it?"

Conan retained his stance. Blood dripped from his neck where the sword was cutting into his flesh.

Jennifer looked into Bran's eyes. She stepped away from Conan.

"You can take me next," Jennifer said.

Bran looked at Conan and Jennifer. He nodded and pulled the sword away.

Bran approached and crouched next to Madeline.

"I know I can bring him back, Bran. I'll do anything. Tell me." She looked at Bran.

"Ciaran is a lucky bastard, isn't he?" Bran muttered. "I need him conscious and able accept his kingship before I take him to the tower. I need a privilege, right now."

"The privilege for this trip was used for Tadgh. Not only that, he was killed by your evil King Sciphil sword. A privilege cannot save him," Conan said.

Bran glanced at Conan. "You're the Host. Do something."

"I'll use my lifetime privilege. I can only use it once, and it can only bring him back for a very brief moment. The rest will be in your hands," Conan said.

"That's good enough."

Conan turned around and sped away.

On the ground, Ciaran stirred and opened his eyes. When he saw Bran, anger crossed his face, but he was too weak to say or do anything. He closed his eyes again.

Madeline grabbed Ciaran's shoulders and shook. "Don't waste the privilege your father sacrificed, Ciaran. Open your eyes and accept what Bran says."

Bran glanced at Madeline and said nothing.

Ciaran winced and opened his eyes.

"Ciaran LeBlanc, I now announce you as King of Eudaiz. Do you accept?"

Ciaran stared at Bran, then he closed his eyes again.

"No, no, Ciaran! Open your eyes. Accept it for me." Madeline shook Ciaran's shoulders again and again. His eyes remained closed. He looked as if he were fading away.

This time it would be forever.

Madeline looked at Bran. A tear rolled down her face.

Bran repeated, "Ciaran LeBlanc, I now announce you as the King of Eudaiz. Do you accept?"

No response from Ciaran.

Another moment went past. Then Ciaran winced. He moaned and opened his eyes again.

Behind them, blood streamed from Zach's nose and ears. He couldn't stand. Ayana and Jo had to hold him up. Zach was sending sound waves into Ciaran's head to wake him.

"I'm going to kill you, Zach," Ciaran murmured.

Madeline bent down so that her face was in Ciaran's clear view. "We exchanged vows, Ciaran. I hope you remember and will honor what you said."

Bran asked again, "Ciaran LeBlanc, I now announce you the King of Eudaiz. Do you accept?"

Madeline shoved in, placing her face in Ciaran's view again. She stared straight into his eyes and waited.

"Yes," Ciaran said.

Before Ciaran slipped away again, Bran pulled Ciaran's left arm up and placed a glowing band around his wrist. The band absorbed into Ciaran's arm and vanished. Bran pulled Ciaran up and zoomed out of the Daimon Gate.

CHAPTER 40

The life force rained down. Ciaran saw waves of magnificent energy flowing into his body. He was floating inside a glass chamber.

This was the king chamber. He was sure of it.

Thousands of light beams crossed and connected to his body. With every moment that passed, an inexplicable energy from the light flew into him. He knew he was receiving the eudqi of his King Sciphil.

His body and his mind flew, floated, and then reformed again.

The energy turned him around. Spinning. Floating. Slowing down.

Now, in the standing position, he could see through the glass panel. He saw Bran standing outside, looking at him.

With every minute, Bran's body deteriorated. As the light beams of energy flew into Ciaran, the same went out of Bran.

Bran's eyes were still strong and sharp. His intense gray eyes pierced through the glass chamber, looking at Ciaran. A proud smile crossed his face.

Ciaran was drawing the life force from Bran. He couldn't stop it. He had accepted the position, and he had no say in the price he was willing to pay.

He hated Bran for what he had done to his mother. But at the same time, a man in Bran's position had saved many lives. He was in charged with an entire universe. There were people who depended on him. He was the king, and that was what it took.

Somehow, Ciaran understood Bran and the motivation for his actions.

If he had decided to take the responsibility at a cost to his family and those he loved, then he was a far greater man than Ciaran could ever be.

He knew his weakness. He was human, and he couldn't let go of his emotions. A tear rolled down Ciaran's face.

"Damn it, that tear you inherited from Conan, not me," Bran cursed.

The transformation process was complete.

Ciaran broke free of the glass chamber. Bran was now no more than a pile of battered flesh, but his eyes were still sharp and intact. He looked at Ciaran.

"I took everything from you, didn't I?" Ciaran said. Another tear rolled down his face.

"Those tears embarrass me, Ciaran. You didn't take anything from me. If I were strong enough, I would be able to retain my physical presence without the eudqi. But I let my body turn to ruin inside the Daimon Gate."

Ciaran reached out for Bran's hand, but Bran's body had started disintegrating.

"I don't have anything to give you as a father but my blood. Remember, the desire for destruction inside you, the violence and the blade of your mind, they come from your Daimon. Do not lose it. It's in my blood. So it's in yours as well. Without destruction, there is no rebirth. It is the principal of life in Eudaiz. It is the virtue of a king. It takes a life to save a life. You don't have to be a righteous man, Ciaran. Not in my realm. But you have to be a just king."

"Don't leave, please. I'm not ready."

"Yes, you are. Conan helped make you the man you are today. Thank him for me. Tell Jennifer I'm sorry for what happened. I did love her. But she belongs to my brother . . ."

Bran's body turned into a pile of dirt that quickly dissolved into the air.

Lost. That was all Ciaran fell at the moment. He was sure it wasn't the feeling Bran had wanted him to have. But he couldn't help it.

He let it be. At the moment, in this king tower, he was by himself. Alone.

He and the multiverse. He gave himself a moment to grieve the father he had never had.

***

Outside the tower, Madeline had just arrived. Ayana had brought her here to wait for Ciaran. Madeline looked at the entrance of the magnificent tower, knowing that Ciaran was inside. She gazed at it as if she might be able to open it with the force of her stare.

The gate swung open. Ciaran walked out in a form as magnificent as Bran had been. He was still her Ciaran. He still looked the same. But he now had the aura of a king.

A tear rolled down Ayana's face. She knew Bran was gone forever.

Madeline knew the only person he saw when he walked out of that gate was her.

Only her.

He strode down the stone steps. She raced toward him. They kissed each other in front of the king tower.

A humming sound approached them. Madeline and Ciaran turned around. Zach, Tadgh, Jo, and Pete arrived in a bizarre looking vehicle.

"Welcome to Eudaiz," Ciaran said as his brother approached hand in hand with Jo.

"Should I call you my majesty?" Tadgh grinned.

Ayana smiled. "We have to go through the coronation process. But it should only be a matter of formality."

"And you will be Sciphil Nine when I am done, Tadgh," Pete said.

Tadgh laughed. "I wish you all the best, and please stay in power as long as possible." Tadgh wrapped his arms around Jo's shoulders. "I assume we can go back and forth between here and Earth, right?"

"Yes, with ease," Pete said.

"Do you intend to go back and take care of LeBlanc Pharmaceuticals, Tadgh?" Ciaran asked and smiled as if he knew the answer already.

"No. I just want to check on Migi and TJ," Tadgh said.

Jo laughed and explained to those who didn't know Tadgh's two very important pets. "Migi is a very cunning cat, and TJ is Ciaran's puppy."

"Please don't refer to TJ as my puppy, Jo. He might take advantage of it," Ciaran chuckled.

They started headed to the vehicle to get to their residence.

"Is the coronation process really going to be just formality?" Madeline asked.

Ciaran shook his head and smiled. Only skeptical Madeline would ask Ayana and Pete that. If claiming the kingship of this multibillion-resident universe was simple, they wouldn't have made the king Sciphil go through such a traumatizing testing process.

But that would be a matter for tomorrow.

For now, he enjoyed the thought of holding their twins in his arms, being with Madeline, and visiting their parents who now resided in the Daimon Gate.

The thought made him smile.

Ciaran and Madeline continue their journey in

MINDSCAPE
Find out more here
http://narrativeland.com/mind

Queen's Gambit
Knight & Pawn
Lone Castle
Doubled Bishops
Dead Squares
King's Endgame

MINDSCAPE 1

CHAPTER 1

Did the gray, dull, and inanimate garden wall in front of her just shiver, sweat, and leak out tears of blood?

This was incredulous. She wasn't Alice in Wonderland. Madeline shook her head. It must be fatigue. She looked at the wall again.

Now, it stood still as any dull gray wall in any backyard. She sighed. It was fatigue.

A strange shade of gray light spread over a garden of plastic-looking trees. Her eyes shot to the sky and widened. She was looking at the magnificent sunset in Eudaiz, a universe far away from Earth.

She smiled.

After what felt like decades of bloodbath and battles, she had survived and come here. The sunset was comforting.

Madeline had read many science fiction novels, which at the moment served the sole purpose of preventing her from freaking out or making a complete idiot of herself.

Then she realized the sunset in front of her was artificial.

The smile left her face, giving way to a frown of anxiety at the daunting thought of an uncertain future.

A few months ago, she would have laughed at the idea that she would ever space travel. But this was worse. She hadn't just space-traveled to get here. She had traveled across dimensions of time and space and God-knows-whatever-else. The sort of travel that didn't allow her to use a map to track the routes, the kind where she didn't know where she had been or how long it had taken her.

In 2015, she had been an accomplished New York journalist. A few short months later, she'd discovered she was not Madeline Roux, but

Madeline Kelley. She was only half human from her mother's side because her father was Eudaizian.

She'd met Ciaran in London and discovered that she could love a man like madness. Ciaran said they were soulmates. But his words were too polished for her. She preferred to say simply that they loved each other. She'd married him a few days ago—in whatever dimension existed between Earth and this place.

She was now Madeline LeBlanc, in whatever year it was in Eudaiz.

Eudaiz was a multi-billion citizen universe, governed by a council of nine Sciphils—a word that stood for Scientist Philosopher. There had been countless times Madeline rolled her eyes internally when she used the term.

In her lay English, she considered the council to be like royalty or a government of some kind. They controlled everything in Eudaiz. What intrigued her most was that the council members were mostly humans who'd come from Earth. A council of nine humans governing an immense universe of alien citizens was a concept she'd never have imagined in her wildest dreams.

The thing was, her grandfather had been Sciphil One. Before he died, he'd appointed her as his successor of the Sciphil One position because she was the last living member of her family. So she was due to take up that appointment in a few days and became Sciphil One. That had been quite a shock to her peaceful life on Earth.

Suddenly her vision wavered. The garden in front of her flickered. "Oh, no," she muttered and turned around to go inside. On Earth, she'd thought she was a pseudo psychic. But since reconnecting with her biological family and accepting this Sciphil One position, her psychic ability had become stronger.

She could see minds and track minds, and sometimes she could even read people's minds. The baggage that came along with that ability was that she had precognition—mostly in regards to negative incidents. They called that her talent. She called it a curse.

She didn't think she could make it back inside the house. It seemed as if the ground was moving under her feet.

On the wall at the other side of the garden, a blood-red text appeared: *ENNEAD WILL KILL YOU ALL.*

The garden bed was covered in blood and gore. Body parts littered the ground.

She wanted to run, but her feet were buried in what looked like bricks made of dried bones. She yanked at her feet but couldn't free them. She called out for Ciaran, but no sound escaped her mouth. The bones built themselves up quickly, now reaching up to her body.

She was suffocating in a tomb of bone.

CHAPTER 2

"**W**elcome home," Kyle Wolf muttered to himself.

Kyle drew in the purified air of Eudaiz to remind himself of what he had missed in his thirty-three years living in exile. He swore to his soul that he would make those responsible for his miseries pay. In this universe—or in the one that contained Earth—his soul was the only possession he was sure was not illusory.

He chuckled at his analogy. As a mind-bender, Kyle's strongest talent was the ability to make others hallucinate. He could control people's minds. And he enjoyed doing it, especially when he made people kill themselves.

The stench of fresh blood always gave him a shiver of pleasure.

Deep in his thought, he tripped on a tub of water. He stared at his reflection in the purified water someone had put out in front of their house to give blessings for the new king of Eudaiz. The face mirrored back at him was a face he hadn't dared to look at for a long time—scarred, wrinkled, and ancient.

He had once possessed the typical angelic, Eudaizian look—and he'd had an innocent Eudaizian mind to match.

Those precious days were long gone.

Eudaiz was a place of happiness where people lived in total contentment and excelled at their individual talents. Eudaizians looked like extraordinarily beautiful humans. People here were born beautiful and saw nothing but beauty in their lives. There was no concept of heaven or hell because those benchmarks just weren't needed. This universe offered its citizens a true happiness that no other universe could.

Kyle cursed to himself and glanced from a distance at the happy crowds preparing for the king's coronation. Only those like him who had visited other universes could understand and appreciate Eudaiz, just as only those who had been to hell would appreciate heaven.

Kyle knew the difference between heaven and hell all too well. Eudaiz was a heaven—a perfect world that had rejected him.

"That should be *my* coronation," Kyle mumbled.

Eudaiz's constitution stated that people deserved happiness when they used their excellence to contribute to virtuous acts. But no one had ever clearly defined what a virtuous act was, and more importantly, what it was not.

Kyle clenched his teeth, thinking of the LeBlancs again. His life's work was down the drain now.

Bran LeBlanc, the previous king of Eudaiz, had cut off his eudqi—the life force that gave him his good looks and invincible strength. And Ciaran LeBlanc. Even the sound of the name made him feel as if his head was going to explode. Ciaran had taken the king's sovereignty. And that would terminate Kyle's existence.

"No!" He couldn't let that happen. "Damn you all. I curse you all," he growled. He whirled around in anger. "Ennead will kill you all. I swear to the gods of darkness, I will make them pay. The ennead will kill them all . . ."

A Eudaizian man carrying a tub of purifying water stepped out from a house and ran straight into Kyle. Half of the water in the tub poured out onto Kyle. Putting the tub down, the man turned to check on him.

He caught Kyle's face and withdrew slightly. Then he spoke politely in Eudaizian, "I apologize."

Kyle smiled. He understood that no one in Eudaiz was as ugly as he now was. Of course, the man was shocked seeing his deformed face. Kyle answered in his native tongue. "It's not a problem. I'm on my way to the Sciphil zone. I shouldn't arrive like this." He pointed at a few leaves and flower petals still hanging from his clothes. "May I use your facility to wash up?"

"Oh, of course. You're from the Sciphil council. My house is your house." The man pushed the door open and invited Kyle in.

Kyle shook his head. Naive Eudaizians should die. Kyle followed the man in and closed the door behind him.

Sensing something unusual, the man turned around and looked at Kyle. Kyle savored the fear in the man's eyes and the pain in his voice when he ripped the man's heart out with his bare hand. Kyle wiped the blood from his hand on the man's clothes.

He moved to the window and peeked outside. The air was filled with the distant sounds of cheering, music, and laughter. The aroma of burnt incense and fresh flowers whirled in the air for a moment and was then whisked away by the wind.

"Long live the king!" he hummed the words in his throat and smirked.

CHAPTER 3

Ciaran searched the garden and found Madeline fainted on the ground. His wife scared the hell out of him sometimes. He could see nothing unusual in the garden. The plantation in the garden looked plastic, but having dealt with chemicals for such a long time, he recognized that the material was organic, just not of Earth.

He knew for sure that the dome above that looked like sky was artificial. Its purpose was to create an environment that a human body could tolerate. The air inside the dome was normal. There were no strange creatures here or anything in the garden that he could peg as a sign of danger. *So why had Madeline fainted?*

He looked back at the house. It was more like a grand mansion than a bunker or a stereotypical space residence. Ciaran smiled to himself. Bran was Irish. It was only natural he'd build such a house to live in.

Ciaran noticed an old robot standing at the corner of the garden and approached it. It hadn't been operated for a long time. If dust existed in Eudaiz, the machine must have gathered a lot of it. He activated the robot.

The machine came back to life. After humming for a second, it blinked and looked at Ciaran. At first, the monitor on its chest was blank. Then it seemed to reconnect to the current network, and it updated its system.

Text appeared on the monitor on the robot's chest. "Please verify your access."

Ciaran pressed his right palm to the control panel.

"Left palm please," the text stated.

Ciaran pressed his left palm to the control panel.

"Welcome to Sciphil Three's residence, Ciaran LeBlanc—king-to-be of Eudaiz," the robot verbalized.

"Is there a surveillance system in this garden? I need to know what happened here before I activated you," Ciaran said.

"Yes. The data is available in your control room," the robot said.

Ciaran nodded and turned to go to the house.

"Please accept my condolences about Bran's death. It was a great loss for Eudaiz," the robot said.

Ciaran paused and looked at the machine. "You are one smart robot."

"My name is Robert. I am the first-generation robot that could potentially handle data from the EYE."

Ciaran glanced around to ensure no one was close by. "I thought you were a garden robot."

"No. I am the central robot. 245.21YZ ago, Bran deactivated me here because he was in haste to leave for a mission."

"How long ago?" Ciaran asked, arching an eyebrow.

"My apologies. Converted into Earth time, it has been the equivalent of thirty-three years since he deactivated me."

"No one has reactivated you since then. How do you know your information is up-to-date?"

"Only a King Sciphil can activate me. You will be King Sciphil in twenty-eight days from now after your coronation. You will have access to the full data of the EYE. My system has been connected to the central databank. It is up-to-date."

Ciaran hissed audibly. He didn't know how much intelligence they had here. How much surveillance data would be available and to whom. Attempting to access the EYE system violated multiversal law and would result in a death penalty.

"We are not authorized to access data from the EYE system. I have no intention of building that databank. Neither did Bran," Ciaran stated as clearly as possible to the robot. He knew the message was being recorded.

"You do not have to worry about surveillance. No one in Eudaiz has the privilege to access King Sciphil's data in his private residence."

Ciaran smiled. *You're a robot. You're allowed to be naive,* he thought. "All right, Robert, how many others have lived in this residence?"

"Pierre LeBlanc until 1655. Aedan LeBlanc until 1755. Ealga LeBlanc until 1805. Malachi LeBlanc until 1976. Bran LeBlanc until 2015. Current owner, Ciaran LeBlanc," the robot narrated the information in a monotone voice.

But every word cut at him like a knife on bone. Generations of his family had been involved in this. And he hadn't known. His parents had worked their whole life to keep him out of it. To spare him the pain of power and responsibility to people he didn't know.

Ciaran LeBlanc, King of Eudaiz. Ciaran shook his head. He wasn't sure how long it would be before he got used to this life. A few months ago, he was a business man, running his family global pharmaceuticals empire out of his London headquarters.

Now he was here, working toward his kingship. There would be a lot to do before his coronation. If claiming the kingship of this universe was easy, there shouldn't have to be much bloodshed required.

He glanced around. Every brick in this place was soaked with the mystery of his family. The mysterious aura that had followed his family for generations. From Earth to the multiverse. Some people considered his family the most mysterious family on Earth.

Perhaps they were right.

He looked at his hands. There was blood on these hands. He'd killed to get here. But as Bran had said, it took a life to save a life. He didn't have to be a virtuous king—he only needed to be a just king.

But would he be capable of being a just king? What would it cost him to do the right thing for the citizens of this gigantic universe?

His emotions were his weakness. He was a human, not a robot. And when it came to his family, he would not compromise. Ever. He would do whatever it took to protect them. Everything else came second to that.

Family!

It dawned on him now why Madeline had fainted.

CHAPTER 4

Madeline was agitated. She needed to tell Ciaran about her precognition. But since Ciaran had found her in the garden, he and the others had made her lie down like a sick puppy. She protested. But then they'd taken a complicated-looking wristwatch off her, and the next thing she knew, she felt as weak as . . . a sick puppy.

At a corner of the room, Ayana Dee, Sciphil Two, and Pete Chandler, Sciphil Nine were talking. They had helped her and Ciaran a lot during the process of coming here. Ayana had been born in Eudaiz. She was as beautiful as an angel. Pete was a British man, recruited later in his life. He was like a kind uncle to Madeline.

Ciaran strode into the hall from a wing of connected corridors. His face was unfathomable—a typical Ciaran expression. He crouched next to her. "How are you feeling?" he asked.

"I'm perfectly fine. I'll feel better if they give me back that wrist unit."

Ciaran nodded toward Ayana, who was holding the wrist unit. She approached and gave the little machine back to Madeline. As soon as she put it on, waves of energy pumped into her body. She felt like a new person. She sat up, but she wasn't sure if she should tell Ciaran about the precognition in front of Ayana and Pete.

After all, she and Ciaran had just arrived in this universe. They didn't know who were friends and who were foes.

"I've taken a look around the residence. Everything looks fine. We can stay here. The top priority for us now is to plan Madeline's officiation as Sciphil One, am I right?" Ciaran asked.

Ayana answered, "Yes, indeed. It is important that she receives her full power in Tower One. Her succession had been authorized and lined up at the precise astronomical time, two days from now. If we fail to officiate her, the power of Tower One will fail—and so will Eudaiz."

"Understood," Ciaran said.

"Let me show you the map." Ayana turned on a floating screen, revealing a map of Eudaiz.

Eudaiz was organized in circles. The towers of power, clearly labeled, stood in a protected area. In the middle was Tower Three, the king tower. The other eight towers were located in a circle surrounding it. They looked like the eight petals of a sunflower.

Ayana pointed to the king tower and said, "This is the core of Eudaiz's power. It must be protected at all costs. The king has access to all towers. However, each Sciphil has access only to their own tower. So, Madeline, after officiation, you will have full access to Tower One. I have full access to Tower Two. And Pete has access to Tower Nine. Ciaran has access to all."

Madeline gestured widely. "So, given how important the towers are, security is critical. This universe has more than six hundred billion citizens. This must be a massive area. How can you guarantee security for the towers?"

Ayana smiled. "The tower zone is called the Sciphil zone. No citizens are allowed in there. The area is self-contained and quite small. The security of the Sciphil zone is strict and has never been breached in five hundred years. The towers have no entry point for anyone except the Sciphil of the tower and the king. Within each tower, there are nine round protective layers—they would spin and grind any unauthorized individuals into dust if they attempted to trespass."

Madeline nodded.

Pete pointed to a large circle which wrapping outside of the Sciphil zone. He said, "This is the Sciphil residential area. Each Sciphil has a residence, located as close to his or her respective tower as possible. We are here, at Sciphil Three residence." He pointed to a dotted line. "The internal capsule is strictly private and secure. It operates only for people with the right access. The capsule terminals are like subway systems in New York or London. So really, within the Sciphil zone and Sciphil residence areas, I wouldn't worry too much about security."

Ayana pointed to a larger circle outside the Sciphil residential area. "This is where the six hundred billion citizens live." The area took up a large area of the map. Ayana continued. "There are eight districts, located in circles in the outer ring here. Each Sciphil governs a district. No citizen has ever been allowed into the Sciphil zone."

"There are nine Sciphils and eight districts. Who doesn't have a district to govern?" Ciaran asked.

"You, Ciaran." Ayana smiled.

Pete laughed. "You have to manage all of the Sciphils and handle important matters such as protecting Eudaiz from our enemies. I think it's only fair to exempt you from the administrative duties of governing a district."

"From what I know, the Black Rock is our number one enemy. Is that information accurate?" Ciaran asked.

Pete shook his head. "No. It's speculative. That universe attacks us all the time because they don't have much energy or natural resources. Other universes may have attacked Eudaiz before, but not during the five hundred years' reign or our Sciphil council. There is no guarantee they won't attack us in the future."

"Have the Black Rock ever breached our security in the Sciphil zone?" Madeline asked.

"No," Ayana responded.

Ciaran nodded. "All right. It's been a long day. I think we should continue this discussion tomorrow."

"It feels as if a day here has fifty hours," Madeline said.

Pete smiled. "We don't use hours. A day here has nine units. Three for the morning, three for the afternoon, and three for the night. Each unit has one hundred slots. At the moment, it is the fiftieth slot of the night. The average person should have at least one unit of sleeping time a day."

Madeline rolled her eyes. Another set of rules and numbers to remember.

"Thank you, Pete. I'll be sure we get enough sleep." Ciaran smiled.

Pete nodded. "Especially you."

Ciaran arched an eyebrow.

Pete continued, "The battles you engaged in before arriving here have drained you of all of your natural energy. In Eudaiz, energy is everything. It's life. Eudqi is a special energy for Sciphils. It's like your blood. However, in your case, you won't receive full power until after your coronation. So right now, your energy is fragile and very temporary. Be sure you take advantage of the resting time so that your body can recharge what's used up during the day."

Ciaran raised a hand in frustration. "What you're saying is that, at the moment, I don't have the natural energy to operate my body. And I have to rely on the eudqi—like batteries?"

"Precisely," Pete smiled.

"So don't pick a fight," Madeline laughed.

"We'd better go to sleep now," Ciaran muttered.

"Not here, I hope," Ayana said.

"Why not?" Ciaran asked.

"This place has been vacant for more than thirty years. It can't be comfortable. Madeline has a fully operational Sciphil One residence. You both have full access," Ayana said.

"Yes, we'll go to Sciphil One residence later. But I'd like to have a bit of time here with Madeline, if we may," Ciaran said.

"It's only for one night. We can manage. If you could stop by again tomorrow and take us to Tower One, it would be greatly appreciated." Madeline smiled.

Ayana nodded. "Very well then. We will let you have some privacy. It's been a long day."

Ayana and Pete left the residence.

Madeline opened her mouth to tell Ciaran about what she had seen in the garden, but before she could say a word, Ciaran had locked his lips with hers. Whenever he engaged in such an intimate act, she was defenseless.

Suddenly, Ciaran glanced toward the side door. "Who's that?" he shouted and darted toward the door, weapon drawn.

For a limited time, D.N. Leo gives away
4 books in the Multiverse Collection

CLAIM YOUR FREE E-BOOKS
http://narrativeland.com

THANK YOU FOR READING!
D.N. LEO

D.N. LEO 'S NOVELS
SERIES READING ORDER

http://www.narrativeland.com/dnleo-series-reading-order

—

A SHADE OF MIND
(narrativeland.com/shade)
Main Characters: Ciaran, Madeline, Tadgh, and Jo
(Recommended reading in order)
1-4 Random Psychic
2-4 Forever Mortal
3-4 Elusive Beings
4-4 Imperfect Divine

—

SPECTRUM
(narrativeland.com/spectrum)
Main characters: Lorcan, Orla, Roy and Mori
(Recommended reading in order)
1-4 White Curse
2-4 Blue Fox
3-4 Indigo Stone
4-4 Red Moon

—

MINDSCAPE
(narrativeland.com/mind)
Main characters:
Ciaran, Madeline, Tadgh, Jo, Kyle, Hoyt, Ayana,
Pete, Sizx, Lorcan, Orla
(Recommended reading in order within series, can
be read in ANY order in related to other series)

Queen's Gambit
Knight & Pawn
Lone Castle
Doubled Bishops
Dead Squares
King's Endgame

—

SILVER BLOOD
Main characters:
(narrativeland.com/silver)
Ciaran, Madeline, Tadgh, Jo, Caedmon, Sedna, Roy,
Mori, Zach, Mya, Lorcan and Orla
This series can be read in ANY order within the
series and in related to other series.

Virgo
Libra
Scorpio
Taurus
Pisces
Gemini

Thank you for reading.

If you enjoyed reading **Imperfect Divine**, I would appreciate it if you would help others enjoy this book, too.

Recommend it. Please help other readers find this book by recommending it to friends, readers' groups and discussion boards.

Review it. Please tell other readers why you liked this book by reviewing it wherever you purchase the book from. If you do write a review, please send me an email at info@dnleo.com so I can thank you with a personal email.

COPYRIGHT

Imperfect divine
A Shade of Mind Series - Book 4

By D.N. Leo